Minnow

MINNOW
James E. McTeer II

HUB CITY PRESS
SPARTANBURG, SC

Hub City Editor: C. Michael Curtis
Cover Illustration: Lucy Davey
Book Design: Meg Reid
Proofreaders: Megan DeMoss, Rebecca Landau and Rachel Richardson
Printed in Dexter, MI by Thomson-Shore

Library of Congress
Cataloging-in-Publication Data

McTeer, James E., II, 1983-
Minnow / James E. McTeer II.
pages cm
ISBN 978-1-938235-11-5 (hardback : alk. paper) —
ISBN 978-1-938235-12-2 (e-book)
 1. Fathers and sons—Fiction.
 2. Diseases—Treatment—Fiction.
I. Title.
PS3613.C67M56 2015
813'.6—dc23
2014034485

Support for the South Carolina First Novel Prize is provided
by the Phifer Johnson Foundation of Spartanburg, SC, and the
South Carolina Arts Commission.

186 West Main St.
Spartanburg, SC 29306
1.864.577.9349
www.hubcity.org | twitter/hubcitypress

For my parents, Thomas and Kathleen McTeer

Minnow watched Varn's scarred lips move as he finished his tale. Minnow had known his friend since before memory, but still winced at the puckered scars on his lips and cheeks.

They took turns telling stories around a small fire in their hideout. The slanting scrap-metal roof was rusted with enough holes to chimney the smoke, but the inside still swirled with a dim haze. Curtains of gray Spanish moss hung down across each open end, keeping out the early morning light.

Minnow had found the place long ago on the edge of a marsh not far from Bay Street. He took the gang there, and they built the hideout together. It was hidden amidst low palmetto fronds and cooled by fresh salty air drifting in from the river.

Martin stole a box of matches so they could have real fires, and they stocked the hideout with treasures: driftwood pieces, rusty scraps pulled from the pluff mud, raccoon skulls uncovered on the bluff. Everett found an old twisted rag that he said was a hoodoo doll, but they buried it away from their territory. Sometimes they brought food and made a picnic, like they were camping in the wild jungle out on the far islands.

Shadows lapped across Varn's scarred face. He had been a baby when he took a tin of boiling grease and tried to drink it like a cup of milk. His top lip was bubbled and shiny, and a raised scar spread from cheek to cheek. Minnow didn't like looking at the scars, so he watched the fire instead. Varn told a story about the Yemassee Indians running settlers out of Newfort long ago and murdering anyone left behind.

"The women and girls who got on the boats had to look back and watch as they sailed away. Their houses and fields were burning. Even some of their babies were burning. They had to watch as their men and boys ran to the water's edge and got caught by the Indians. The Indians skinned them alive, and the women and girls could hear it as they sailed off. They could hear their menfolk screaming for help and could smell their skin crackling like bacon."

Varn took something out of his pocket and licked his scars.

"You know what this is?"

He opened his hand and showed a big arrowhead in his palm. It was as long as Minnow's index finger. Gray. Sharp.

"This is from a Yemassee arrow. It lodged in someone's skull. Probably one of those men who was screaming so loud."

Minnow gazed at the arrowhead and then looked up at Varn. Minnow had found arrowheads before. They looked a lot like Varn's. None of them had come from a skull. He wondered if Varn's really had.

"Is that true?" Martin asked. He was the youngest of them, just six, and he'd scooted away from the fire when Varn got to the scalping.

"It's true the Yemassee ran everyone off," Minnow said.

Varn scowled and sliced the arrowhead through the air like a knife.

"You're scared, too."

"It was a good story," Minnow said.

Varn crossed his arms and smiled. He was the biggest and the oldest, almost twelve years old.

"Did an Indian really scalp someone with it?" Martin asked.

"Of course not, stupid. Who knows? It was probably from a deer hunt. Here."

He tossed it at Martin, but the boy recoiled and it landed in the dirt by the fire.

"I don't want it," Martin said, looking down at the point.

"Leave it in the box," Everett said, but Minnow held his hand out.

"I'd like it, for a while."

Varn nodded.

"Fine. Maybe you'll run into an Indian on your way home. But bring it back."

Minnow took the arrowhead. It was flint, with a wicked flare, but the butt of it was thick and sturdy in his grip.

"I gotta go," Martin said, pulling back the nearest curtain of moss to let in a few bars of sunshine. "I told Ma I'd be back by noon."

Minnow squinted at the light. The sun was well up. Martin was in trouble, because noon was close. They'd come early that morning, before sunrise and the heat of the day. Martin left, and Everett followed him.

"That was a good story," Minnow told Varn.

Varn looked at the fire. "I'll stay and watch it burn out. You go. I know you have to."

"Thanks."

Minnow went around him and stopped at the moss curtain.

"It's a nice arrowhead," he said.

"Yeah. I hope your papa's all right."

Minnow nodded and went out into the bright world.

HIS FATHER'S BODY LAY ON A BED. Almost no life remained under the second skin of white sheet. Minnow stood in front of the only window in the room, watching his father take shallow breaths. Waxy glass let in diffuse light from the blue summer sky, but the room shook with shadows cast by tapers wasting away under hot little fires. Darkness drew across a faded portrait of Minnow's grandfather in a gray uniform.

He shared the air with his father. The dust. Maybe that sick taste from his father lying there a month, being washed as much as possible, but not nearly enough. The room was almost dead, with just small pieces of life left inside.

He moved so he wouldn't freeze there forever. He moved only as close as he would have gotten if the man had been awake. His father slept, eyes closed, lips pursed as if whistling, cracked and dry. The skeleton beneath the blanket wasn't really his father but a wraith left behind. That thing couldn't work. That thing couldn't sing, or dance, or tell a story.

"It's Minnow."

He reached his hand out with two fingers extended, but then stopped. His mother walked in, and he withdrew his hand.

She crossed the room and put a bowl of something next to the bed. She perched on the edge and looked down at Minnow's father but didn't say a word. She was wearing her favorite white dress. The one with blue flowers.

"Just because he can't talk doesn't mean you shouldn't," Minnow said.

"He never liked talking much anyway," she said.

"But you'd like talking to him."

She nodded and put a hand on his stubbly cheek.

"You hear your son? Taking care of me?"

Minnow stepped back, glanced at the door.

"Stay."

He stayed.

"It isn't working," she said.

The boy looked at his father.

"I know."

"The doctor knows something that might help. For his lungs. His breathing."

"Did you get it?"

"Not yet."

"Let me go."

She shook her head. "It's right in town. I'll go. It's not yours to do."

"I can't do anything but watch. Let me go," Minnow said.

She gave him one of his father's old leather billfolds, just a scrap of hide, and put a dollar in it with a piece of paper. She folded it for him. He put it in his pocket and pressed it down. More money than he'd ever had at once.

"You got to go to Ander's for it."

"On Bay Street."

"Right on Bay Street. You get it, get yourself a soda if you can, and come home."

She pressed down his hair with the same hand she'd touched his father with. The shaggy hair, sandy-colored like his father's once was, covered his eyes. She smiled.

"Talk to him," Minnow said. "Tell him what you did today. Maybe what you dreamed last night. I'll tell him about my trip when I get back, and he'll feel strong hearing our voices."

She looked away and then looked back. She straightened the loose collar on Minnow's summer shirt and leaned down to brush nothing off his chest and stomach.

"You didn't learn to talk like that around here," his mother said. "Where did you come from, boy?"

"From you."

He left them in the quiet room.

Minnow emerged from the house into the afternoon sun. It was a South Carolina summer, hot and humid. The heat hit his nerves and gave him life. No time to waste. His mother needed him, and his father. If things went well, he'd be getting a soda, too.

He paused on the stoop to catch a breath of air and then crossed the dry, crackling grass to the road out front. He stopped on the verge and turned. A bigger trip might mean a brown sack with lunch in it. A trip out to the Island would mean a fishing pole or maybe a good walking stick. This was just downtown, though, just south to the river.

He hesitated again and then returned across the yard to the stoop for his summer shoes. They were only barely holding together—a few scraps of leather connected by his mother's careful stitches—but they would add some protection to the thick padding his feet developed over the hot months when shoes were mostly negotiable.

The road took him away from his house and his neighbor's shack and past a few old shanties on the corner. He waved at Mrs. Marcy, bent over her splintered picket fence, looking for anyone to talk to.

The road to town from his house was a familiar route, and today its sights and sounds were a sideshow to the main event. He had a dollar, and everyone back home was depending on him. Even if he saw any of the gang, they'd have to wait. They wouldn't understand. They'd want to spend some of the money on candy, which might not be such a bad idea some other time. But not today.

He passed Mr. Jack's inn, the first inn on the way to town, overflowing onto the porch with boarders. He passed the main stable for the Avery phosphate operation, smelling like hay and horse manure. He passed a tabby hovel where an old negro lived with his cat. The man made bread in an oven out back and sold it to people for cheap.

An oxcart passed him, the ox with horns wider than the cart. A little man sat on the driver's seat, hauling a load of seed rice, headed away from town. A pair of men—probably sailors—passed on the other side, going the same direction.

Another oxcart passed, and another, and then Minnow caught up with a strolling couple and overtook them. They looked like they lived on Bay Street and were just out enjoying the afternoon. The man had a pocket watch on a chain and a fancy hat, and she had a hat and a silk parasol. It was a nice day for a walk: hot but clear, cooler in shady places where spidery live oaks put their moss-draped arms across the road, or where palmetto trees spread wide emerald fans to sway in the river breeze.

The dirt road widened, and he left the roadway to walk the brick path that wound alongside. He passed tall white houses with broad porches and went by the Episcopal church that his family had patronized generations ago when they had had more money and lived closer to the river. The white church had a grand steeple, and the whole place was surrounded by a tall wrought-iron fence.

Minnow walked into town, where low brick buildings were topped by white clapboard dwellings and a grid of dirt roads led past shops and stores and offices. He heard a party in a courtyard behind a gray tabby wall. People clinked glasses and women laughed over their husbands' voices. Horses clopped down side streets, and a mule brayed somewhere toward Bay Street and the river. The air smelled sweet, like the heady perfume of yellow jasmine flowers. Farther along he caught a whiff of something fruity and warm, like maybe a lady in one of the upstairs apartments baking a Saturday pie.

He walked onto Bay Street, paved in cobblestones and flanked by the premier businesses of town. Locals and travelers alike walked up and down the wide street between horses and oxcarts. People talked and shopped under awnings and in the shade of buildings, trying to find respite from the sultry summer air.

His favorite store was Roth's, the candy store all the way down on the corner. He liked the soft candy gumdrops and peppermint sticks and the way they mixed a soda just right. It would take longer to walk all the way down there, though, and his main concern today was time.

He stayed close to the front of the shoe store on the near side of the road, watching people pass. Summer brought the planters in from the islands to escape the heat and the yellow fever. They strolled with their wives and children, spending money at whatever shops they liked. Sailors and seafarers walked the street, too, come in to town from Port Royal. You couldn't buy civilized things like fancy clothes or a cream soda in Port Royal, so they left that rowdy place to do their business in town. He saw a few kids. No one he knew, really, except a little boy from school. None of his gang. Even if they were around, they'd just slow him down.

He slipped in behind a stinky ox and followed its cleared path down Bay Street, avoiding the milling crowd. He crossed and stood in the shade of the buildings on the other side, then walked with his hands in his pockets past store-fronts and shop doors.

He got to Ander's but stopped in the alley first. He walked down, just barely able to fit broad-shouldered through the brick passage. A salty breeze blew over him when he exited on the other side.

The Newfort River wound behind Bay Street, reaching almost up to the back of the buildings. The wide band of water was calm, barely rippled, cobalt blue under a bright sky, bordered on both sides by fields of powder-green marsh grass. Boats and dinghies and a few bigger barges cruised up and down the living water. The main ferry from Bay Street to the Island was midway on its course, with old Calico urging his rowers at their work. A negro on a flat-bottom raft cast a spinning net at the edge of the marsh on the opposite side.

A few children played down on the slimy rocks that acted as a barrier between the river and Bay Street buildings. It wasn't a bad place to spend the day, but Minnow did not have time for an adventure. He returned to Bay Street and didn't stop to watch the crowd. His father was in bed, back home, waiting.

Ander's was one of the stores with a big glass front that showed what was going on inside. A few people were up at the soda bar, and a few people shopped at the shelves of general goods. Minnow eyed the man behind the counter, straightened his shirt, and went inside.

HE PUSHED THROUGH THE DOOR, and the young couple at the soda bar looked back. A little bell jingled, and the shoppers exited behind him. The man behind the counter kept his head down, checking something on a piece of paper. Minnow looked left, at the groceries, then right at the bar. All the candy and soda and novelties were behind the bar, at the man's back. The medicine was farther down. Usually Minnow was there with his mother, picking up her foot ointment, but he'd never been alone. The place smelled like the ointment.

He walked the length of the bar, past the couple, and the man turned his eyes up and watched him go. He had greased-back black hair, and his forehead was tall and smooth. He looked back down at the paper. Minnow stopped and stepped up to the counter, his head barely rising over the burnished wooden edge.

The shelves were nine-high from floor to ceiling, stacked with bottles, cans, and jars. Most were labeled, some were not. A few items he didn't recognize: a wooden device, a metal thing with a flat round head, a bundle of leather strips. Many things appeared as if they'd been there for a long time, dust-covered and piled up, almost spilling off the edge.

Another customer came in. The man behind the counter looked up and then glanced over to see Minnow standing there.

"You looking for something in particular?"

The man set his pencil down and walked over. He stopped to check something that Minnow couldn't see on the back shelf, and then continued down slowly, as if he knew the need was urgent but still would take his time.

Minnow reached down and took out the wallet and spread it wide to retrieve the dollar and the prescription. He fumbled the bill and it fluttered down to his feet to the floor. He bent down and scooped it up, and as he straightened he noticed the two teenagers at the bar looking at him.

"You need something?" the man asked.

Minnow looked up and his face was hot. He wiped his hand across his brow and then set his palm on the bar surface, wrist bent and forearm hanging vertically.

"Don't take that out in here if you don't need something. Lots of people like a dollar to spend."

"Yessir."

Minnow set the prescription down on the bar with his free hand and slid it toward the pharmacist. The man took it, unfolded it, read it, wrinkled his brow, and looked up at Minnow.

"Somebody's sick in their lungs."

"Yessir."

"Who's sick? Your momma?"

"My father, sir."

"What's he got?"

"He's been sick a long time."

"With what?"

Minnow shook his head.

The man put a hand to his chin, clicked his teeth together. "Fever?"

"Some."

"I don't have this," the man said, and pushed the paper back.

"What do you mean?"

The man leaned in closer to Minnow's head.

"We don't have it. I don't carry it. Never have. Who prescribed this?"

"I don't know, sir."

"Doctor?"

"Yessir."

"What doctor?"

"I don't know," Minnow said, and licked his lips. His forehead felt hot again. He just wanted to help his parents. Help them, and get a soda. "A man with dark hair, like yours. He's tall. He comes sometimes to see my father."

"Tall?" the man asked, and smiled. "Well, that clears it up. Doesn't it?"

Minnow studied the wood grain of the bar. A black circle was there, like from a cigarette ash.

"Do you know who might have it?" Minnow asked.

The pharmacist frowned and shook his head. One of the teenagers finished a soda, and the straw made a sucking sound that filled the whole place.

Minnow wiped his forehead again. His mother back home. Father in bed. Waiting on him. He couldn't even get a soda. How could he get a soda if he couldn't bring back the medicine?

"What about the one on the Island? What about the one who works out there?"

"He works out there, boy, but he gets all his medicine from me. No one around here has got it."

Minnow swallowed.

"You need anything else?" the man asked.

Minnow looked into the back of the store, then up toward the glowing window at the front. The teenagers got up and left. The bell jingled as the door clapped shut. The bright sound faded fast, along with all of his plans to return triumphant. They were alone in the store.

"No sir."

He put the dollar in the billfold, folded the prescription, put it back too, and then folded the whole thing into his pocket.

"You need anything else?"

"No sir."

"Go see your mama and tell her she can't get that outside of Savannah. Don't know what fool wrote it."

He nodded and walked down the length of the bar past the dirty soda glasses. He squinted at the light outside and could see people passing like ghosts, warbled and dizzy in the wide field of glass. The heat on his forehead passed, now, and he stopped at the door.

He set his hands on the door and pushed it open, looking up at the bells as they rang.

"Boy."

He stopped with the door still open. The musty air of the shop blew past him into the hot street. Minnow didn't turn around when he answered. His father would have whipped him for that, probably.

"Yessir?"

"Boy, come here."

He closed the door and walked over. He approached the edge of the counter, and the man sighed and put his elbow down. He leaned in.

"I know one man who might have it."

Minnow jerked his head up and stared the man in the eyes. "Who is it?"

"He's a type of doctor."

"Where?"

"Near here."

"Please tell me who it is. My father's very sick."

"He can sell you that paste for half that dollar."

"Where is he?"

"Give me the other half."

"Sir?"

"You don't need it all. Give me half and I'll tell you where to go to make your daddy all better."

Minnow looked down at his shoes. He had a dollar. For medicine and a soda. But if the medicine was less, he could skip the soda and his mother wouldn't be mad, and it would be the same, really.

He dug the billfold out and flung it open, spilling the dollar onto the bar. The man laughed and clapped one hand over the bill and dragged it across the wood until it dropped off the edge into his other hand. He took two quarters from a pocket on his apron and put them on the wood. They rang dully, and one spun in a circle before it lay flat.

"You can get it at a place in Port Royal."

Minnow took a step back and raised his eyebrows.

"Port Royal?"

"Yes."

"No doctors are there."

Sailors, fighters, travelers, and thieves—but no doctors.

"I'm thinking of one you don't know about. Or maybe you do."

Minnow stood there, arms limp. He shook his head.

"Doctor Crow works out of Port Royal. Last of his kind. At least this far in."

"Doctor Crow?"

"Crow."

"He comes to town sometimes," Minnow said.

"You know him then."

"He has purple glasses. So he can see inside your soul."

The pharmacist laughed.

"You believe in hoodoo, boy?"

"No sir. I mean, I've never seen much of it, so I don't believe so."

The man leaned in farther, this time close enough that Minnow could smell tobacco on his tongue.

"Don't let him put the root on you, boy. You give him that money and get what you need and get out of there, or you'll wake up a stud boar out past the Island with negroes spear-hunting you."

Minnow shook his head.

"You're sure he has it?"

"He's got lots. You go find out."

"Where do I find him?"

"Down by the oyster rake. He's got a place there."

"What do I tell him?"

"You don't tell him nothing. You give him that paper, and that money, and he'll give you what you need. And you most certainly don't tell him who sent you there. You got it?"

"Yessir."

"Now you need anything else from me?"

"No sir."

"If you come back here, it better be for a good reason."

"Yessir."

Minnow left the pharmacy for Bay Street. His billfold was lighter, but he'd found a way. He practically skipped away from the store, down the line of shops, weaving in and out of people on the street. Martin hollered from the opposite side, waving a dirty hand in the air. Minnow turned and waved but didn't stop. A rolling wagon blocked their sight of each other, and then Martin was lost in the crowd again.

Minnow stopped at the end of the shops, where Bay Street widened and the stores ended, and only a few smaller buildings dotted the downtown boundary. The land dropped away farther up the road, falling into a steep grass bluff that overlooked the marsh and the river. Enormous live oaks towered from the bluff, holding their long arms out over the water as if to cool their leaves. White mansions stood opposite the trees on the other side of the lane: true mansions with wide porches and tall columns.

He looked down Bay Street, busy and hot, and then up the shady bluff road. Port Royal was a half-hour walk, probably, way down the bend. He'd never been there, not even with his mother or father. Not with the gang, not with anybody. Only sailors went to Port Royal, and people who did business with sailors.

Half-hour down, half-hour up. He could run some of the way back if he felt it, and his shoes held. His heart thrummed in his chest, and he started walking.

The road led him past the mansions where planters came to escape the swamps in summer. That's what his father told him: that more colored folks than white folks were out on the islands this time of year, working the farms, tending gardens, taking care of things. He passed the houses and followed the road as it led along the bluff's edge. He gazed out over the river. Bay Street was off to his left, but way ahead down the wide river he could see the faded gray shape of Port Royal. Boats were anchored right off the bluff, and a little farther out, all manner of craft moved up and down the waterway.

The broad vista of the river dropped from view, and he walked down the narrow road, turning gently to the left as the path followed the now-hidden river. The forest around him fell silent except for squirrels dashing through the understory around him. Now and then an oxcart came, moving between town and the port, carrying people or cargo or animals or a little bit of everything. Men rode by on horses in single file, but he was the only one who traveled alone, and on foot.

The trees narrowed the road to a one-man path. A cart came, and he had to step into the woods to avoid being run down. He walked on, and the forest mixed with skinny water oaks and low saw palmettos that formed a solid underbrush. Pine trees stood like sentinels in the earth, limbless until high in the canopy where they stretched out their needle-spiked branches. The trunks leaked sap like orange blood, and the air smelled like sweet peppermint pine. The trunks caught the slightest breeze, and they swayed and groaned. He thought of the ghost stories his gang told at the hideout. The headless horseman. The golden arm. The hand. He'd never walked the forest road, never seen these woods. It was another world, even just out from town.

The pines thinned and became sparse, and soon he could see through the trees again. He saw a log cabin in one spot. Another overgrown clearing showed old stone ruins like blunted teeth jutting from the floor of rotting pine needles. He passed a shanty and then an old campsite visible from the road. Charred tin cans ringed an ashy fire pit. The road widened and the trees fell away to allow two flanking ditches. He walked in one of the dry ditches, off the road, looking out into the trees. He let his eyes drift to the needles at his feet, and when he looked up, he was there.

The trees let go, and the land cleared to show more houses and shacks clustered outside the busy port. Caravans and people gathered in clearings, preparing to set off down the road. He crouched on the edge of the woods and surveyed the place he was forbidden to go. It didn't look too bad.

The buildings went out in front of him, growing taller and thicker until they formed another town, another village on the river. The town's structures had been whitewashed once, perhaps, but now the place was gray and dusty and smeared with mud and soot. He could not see the river or any sign of water from the forest path.

Minnow walked past a courtyard formed by three squat houses. Bare-chested men sat on the stoops, some drinking from dark brown bottles, some smoking and sending white spirals from their lips. Another man stood at the center of the courtyard by a table. He was barefoot and wore loose gray slacks. He had a cigarette in his mouth and something like a machete in his hand. He chopped up and down at a long silver fish with its mouth hung open and one clear yellow eye shining in the sun. A negro took the cut parts of the fish and separated them into baskets. The negro's hands were covered in platinum fish scales that coated his dark skin to the elbows. Minnow felt their eyes tracking him as he walked by, moving deeper into the port. He kept his eyes down and tried not to be noticeable. His stomach twisted, and he gritted his teeth.

The salty air carried sounds of clanking rigging from somewhere past the buildings. He passed a tavern and an inn, both completely wooden and boarded up so he couldn't see anything inside. He could hear music from a tinny instrument, and he could hear the sound of boots clomping against wood. The rest was a mystery.

An open juke joint showed its insides through a wide door and thin-slatted windows. Women danced inside with men, and someone turned an organ that spurred a little monkey into a jig. The monkey smoked a cigarette while the organ grinder laughed.

A dog barked nearby and brought his attention out of the dance hall and back onto the path. Up ahead a long, low building sat perpendicular to his route. It was divided into sections, five in all, but had no doors on the side Minnow approached.

He followed the muddy, trodden path past a rotting pile of fish guts toward the side of the building. A man screamed somewhere off to his right, many blocks away. Minnow looked over his shoulder at how far he had come from the road. His palms were sweaty. He could still turn back.

The other side of the long building had the doors, and each had a stoop. One or two of the places seemed abandoned. Another was a burned shell. A rooster wandered inside the ruined place, pecking at debris on the floor. Three men sat in front of one house. One on the stoop, two flanking. One of them smoked a cigar butt as fat as a quarter but no longer than a fingernail. All of them had beards and leathered faces burned by the sun. The one on the right spoke.

"What are you doing here?"

Minnow took a few more steps before he realized who the man was talking to. He stopped and turned to face them. His cheeks felt hot.

"I'm just here for a while."

"I didn't ask how long you were here. I asked why."

"I'm here to get something. I've got something to buy."

"Something to buy?"

The man on the right stood up. His two partners stayed still, except for the one who moved to take an occasional puff on his cigar.

"What have you got to buy?"

"My father is sick," Minnow said. Maybe his story would give the man pause. Minnow tapped his foot once, to test his muscles. The man stopped to bend over and adjust his shoe. Minnow glanced over his shoulder at the road. Pretty clear. Lots of places to hide, but he didn't know the port at all.

"No doctor here."

"I've got one to see."

The man stopped again, this time just looking. A few steps more, and he'd be too close.

"Who you seeing?"

"Dr. Crow."

All three men burst out laughing. The man with the cigar relented and put it out in the dirt next to him. The talking man slapped his leg, leaned in, and stood up with a smile across his face.

"Dr. Crow? You going to Dr. Crow for what?"

"Medicine."

"Don't you know who that crazy old man is?" the cigar man asked.

"What you going to buy? A magic spell?" the first man added.

"I was sent here. By the man at Ander's."

"He sent you here? How much money you give him?"

"Fifty cents."

"You got more?"

"It's for the medicine."

"Don't give that old negro any money," the cigar man said, and leaned in and whispered to his silent friend. Then he looked back at Minnow and licked his lips. "Give it to me."

"I just want to see him and get what I need."

A foghorn bellowed out on the river. He could taste the salt water.

"Does your mama know you're here, boy?"

Minnow shook his head.

"Anyone know you're here?"

Another shake.

Cigar man stood up.

"Maybe we ought to tell someone. You don't need to be messin' around with no old negroes."

Minnow stepped away and the man appraised him, up, down. The third man on the stoop stood up.

"You think you're up to it?" talking man asked.

"Yessir."

The man nodded.

"He's just a crazy old man. Negroes love him, but he ain't worth much."

"Can you tell me where to find him?"

"He's down by the oysters. Got a shack."

"The oysters?"

"Up from the docks is a muddy place. Big oyster rake. The oysters. You'll see his shack. Go to the river and follow it up."

Minnow nodded.

The other two men came closer.

"Don't come back this way."

Minnow nodded and took a few backward steps before turning and walking away. He glanced back once and the men were standing closer together, the cigar man talking, all three watching him go.

THE ROADS BETWEEN THE BUILDINGS narrowed into tight paths. He walked through mud, stumbling at times to avoid slow-rolling carts and wagons. He passed warehouses: big, wide. Wooden planks had turned black with age, molding in spots where the sun could not reach. A few buildings sent spirals of black smoke up from metal-barrel chimneys. Then the land disappeared.

Docks stretched out like dirty fingers over the flat, gray river. Walkways led out—narrow, gapped, no railings—and terminated at dock-heads stuck out over the water on high pilings. Barnacles crusted the lower reaches where the tide would rise. Some docks had floats at their ends, accessible by ramps that would tilt as the float rose on the incoming tide. Twice each day the tide cycled, rising from a muddy bottom to a high nine feet of water, lifting floats held in place by pilings stuck through galvanized rings.

Shrimp boats took up most of the dock space: bows long and low in the water, arrayed with nets and tackle. Barges moored between the docks hid the water and gave the appearance that the whole place was planked over. Everything moved in the breeze. Boats rocked on their moorings and threatened to jostle down smaller craft.

Men walked up and down the docks from boats and barges to offload their cargo or load supplies. People came off ferries from Charleston and Savannah, and maybe even from farther ports in places like Florida or Maine. The sailors called out: strange men with braided beards, men with pale blonde hair, men with skin as dark as coal, men whose faces had turned brown and freckled by long days at sea. They might have come from The Caribbean, or Mexico, or Africa, or beyond.

Minnow walked down the beach to where the mud met the water, mixing sand and shell. No marsh in this place, where the port had taken everything. Across the river, though, there was a wide field of green marsh, and beyond that a dark wall of trees showing the south face of the Island. The river would lead to Bay Street and off to the open sound. He walked along the shore, watching the water lap at the mud. It was clear for a few feet at the edge, and then it dropped off into murky gray far out under the sky. The sand turned shelly, packed with crumbled white oyster shells like bone fragments set in the ground. The oyster rake spread out before him: wide and long, covering the beach from that point until he could no longer see. The gentle river waves broke against the bleached shells. The oyster halves crunched under his shoes, but some had sharp edges that did not give and would have cut a bare foot like a razor.

The shack stood above the oyster line. He could see neither door nor sign of occupancy. It was a shack made of black boards, with a rough shingle roof. He left the water's edge and circled the shack. It was tiny, no more than a tool shed, and the door faced where Bay Street would be, pointed away from both the river and the port. He saw no sign of any living thing there. What if the shack were empty, abandoned, hopeless?

The closed door hung on rusty hinges. The planks were dark and moldy, but the door was painted fresh and clean in the color of a robin's egg. The cool blue was like a cloudless sky in the afternoon, free of any blemish or shadow. Minnow circled until he stood in line with the blue door. A gull swooped over his head and then rose on a thermal to glide across the river's edge, looking for a fish or a shrimp.

Minnow took a step forward.

"You come a long way today."

He knew it was Dr. Crow. He could tell the person was old, with the rattling voice of an ancient man.

"You come a long way to see me."

Minnow nodded without turning, and then slowly moved on his heels to face the doctor. Before he was all the way around Dr. Crow was walking at him, brushing past in long strides. He had on a faded black suit with a gray undershirt and a hat with a circular black brim. Glasses with purple lenses hid his eyes.

Dr. Crow stepped to his door, made a few moves with his hands around the jamb, and then used a small key on a hidden lock. He opened the door but hesitated before entering the darkness inside.

"You came all this way. So aren't you coming in?"

Minnow nodded, but Dr. Crow was already in his shack, faded from the sunlight like a ghost.

M innow felt the money in his pocket and heaved in a great breath. He thought about his mother and his father back home. The sun was at its apex, risen from the hot morning to blaze down like a torch over the Lowcountry. Midday had come and now slowly diminished, and his mother would wonder why he'd taken so long on Bay Street. Maybe she'd even consider looking for him, leaving his father's side.

He entered the shack and had room to stand only because of its neatness. It was dark and dusty, with only a crack of a window up at the top of the wall that faced the river. Dr. Crow sat in a chair in one corner, with his back to a set of great tall shelves that spanned the wall and reached to the ceiling. A little coal stove with a pipe poked out the side wall, before which Minnow saw a short table, a stool, and a cupboard. The place smelled like desiccated wood. Like an ancient relic pulled from the dry earth.

Dr. Crow sat there with an unlit cigarette in his hand. He held an unstruck match in the other, and he stayed frozen, looking at Minnow.

"You a brave one to come in here. They tell you about me?"

"A few sailors told me the way."

"But that's not who sent you."

"No sir."

"But who sent you told you not to tell."

"I'm not supposed to."

"You supposed to talk to crazy negroes like me?"

"I talk to who I like to talk to. Nobody's out. Not at first, at least."

"Your daddy know that?"

"My father's sick and wouldn't care."

"I know he sick."

"Yessir."

"And you need medicine."

"Yessir."

Dr. Crow struck the match against his shoe and lit the skinny cigarette. He pursed his brown, wrinkled lips and inhaled. The match's sulfur burned Minnow's nose, but the cigarette gave a soothingly pungent vanilla aroma.

"Who told you I had it?" Dr. Crow asked.

"I told him I wouldn't say."

"A man at the pharmacy. In town."

Minnow looked out the door, then back at Dr. Crow.

"On Bay Street?" Dr. Crow asked.

Minnow stayed still.

Dr. Crow blew a stream of smoke out of his mouth. His lips opened, and he laughed. The dry, loud laugh filled the shack. It turned into a cackle that trailed off into a sigh.

"He make you pay for it?"

"No one in town had the medicine."

"I mean to find me. He take your money?"

"Some of it. But I have more."

Minnow dug his fingers into his pocket, but Dr. Crow held his own spidery hand out before Minnow could get the billfold. The palm was light brown, fingers like brown bones, the cigarette pinched between two long digits. The smoke from the tip curled in semicircles before disappearing into the shadows at the ceiling of the shack.

"Don't get no money out in here. I won't take it."

"Please."

Minnow pulled the billfold out and produced the prescription and the quarters. He held the prescription in his hand. It slipped from his fingers and Dr. Crow shot his other hand out, snatching it from the air. He put the cigarette in his mouth and unfolded the sheet.

Minnow held the quarters out in the palm of his hand.

"I have this. It's for the medicine. Please." He looked at the shelf behind Dr. Crow. The vials and canisters did not look like the ones in Ander's. Some seemed handmade: leather pouches clasped with snaps, little glass jars pasted with faded brown labels. Cans half-rusted. One had a label of a knight and said "St. John The Conqueror." Scented tapers, burned stubs, candles cased in tall glasses. Little clay shapes and lumps of stone sat in lines.

"Do you have it?"

Dr. Crow took a final pull from the cigarette and dropped it on the dirt floor. He stepped on it with his shoe. He nodded.

"I don't want your money."

"It's as good as any."

Dr. Crow looked up from the prescription. He refolded it without looking down again and set the paper next to him on the low table.

"Have a seat, boy," he said, and moved to the open door. He closed it and the place fell into darkness. Minnow did not move. A gull squawked outside and men made noises at the docks. Faded shapes showed as his eyes adjusted to the dim light from the crack overhead.

"Have a seat," he repeated.

Dr. Crow lit another match and the flame burned hot and bright for a moment, illuminating the room in gold. A mask hung on the wall, made of a horseshoe crab shell, painted in strange colors and patterns. Dr. Crow lit a candle and then pointed at the stool.

Minnow sat down and clasped his fingers tight around his coins.

Dr. Crow moved across the room to the cabinet and opened a drawer. He took out a stack of paper and then sat down in his chair. The wax melted on the candle and the wick burned brighter. Dr. Crow was still only a shadow, with the flickering light reflected in his purple glasses.

"You see this?" he asked, and held up the paper. Only it wasn't paper. It was money, in a loose bundle. Minnow swallowed and nodded.

"You seen this much?"

Minnow shook his head.

"It's more than your daddy makes in years."

Dr. Crow slipped a dollar from the stack and held it over the candle. The heat of the flame drafted the edge up and then it caught, burning a strange blue color in the dark room. Smoke peeled off as it burned, and the bill curled upward toward the steady, bony hand. Dr. Crow held it until only the smoldering edge remained, and then he let it drop to the floor. He put the stack of money on the low table and turned to Minnow.

"Now what you want to do with them quarters?"

"Please. I can give you the money and anything else I have. I can do anything you need."

Dr. Crow laughed again, the same laugh that started low and then rose into a sharp cackle that seemed sharper with the door closed.

"What can you do that I can't have done for me by some-one who don't come without permission?"

Minnow sucked his bottom lip between his teeth and stared at the candle flames.

"I'm from town. I know it back and forth, sir. I know the Island too."

"Oh, you know the Island."

"I know some of it."

"You know some of it."

Minnow nodded.

"I fish out there. My father took me hunting near Frogmore once."

Dr. Crow tilted his head.

"Hunting for what?"

"Ducks. He got invited out once, to hunt. We had a good time."

Dr. Crow nodded.

"You been out there alone?"

Minnow shook his head.

"No sir. But I could go."

"You think so?"

"I came here on my own."

Dr. Crow's head turned just slightly toward the door.

"I know you did. And now you're alone."

"Please."

Dr. Crow leaned back and gestured at the shelves.

"I don't got what you need."

"What?" The word tasted sour in Minnow's mouth, like vomit.

"I don't got it. But I can get it. Real easy."

"Please." Minnow held out the coins. His eyes struggled, and he saw just two faded rings of silver in his palm. The candlelight showed Dr. Crow's features, but the man stayed still like a statue, one leg crossed over the other.

"You keep that for your quest. You gonna need it."

"Quest?"

"You gonna take a journey."

"To where?"

Dr. Crow stood up and took a jar from the shelf. He set it on the low table next to the candle. The yellow label had long faded away, and the jar was empty.

"You gonna bring me something."

"Sir?"

"You said you could do anything for me. Ain't that what you said?"

"Yessir."

"Then you gonna bring me something I can't get myself, by nature of what it is."

"I'll do anything."

Dr. Crow smiled and Minnow could not see his teeth because they were blackened with rot.

"You ever hear of Sorry George?"

"No sir."

"Let me tell you about Sorry George, and you listen, and when I'm done you decide what you want to do. I can't tell you what to do, but I can tell you this."

Minnow nodded.

"Sorry George lived out past the Island. You know it goes way out, lots of islands, down to tiny hummocks that ain't really islands at all. Just a lump of sand grown up out of the mud, maybe without even one tree growing on it. Sorry George lived out there on one of those islands, and he was a lot like me. But he was different, too. They say Sorry George was the best root doctor ever worked. He was the great-grandson of a slave brought over in chains on a boat from Spain called *Espiritu*. That boat brought two hundred men, but his great-granddaddy was the only witch doctor among them. Warriors, kings, princes. But only one spirit man. So his great granddaddy passed his mantle down to his granddaddy, and then his granddaddy to his daddy, and then his daddy to him.

"So Sorry George practiced out there on them little islands, way out there, and people came from all over to get his help. Only he didn't make all his money helping. Plenty of doctors was helping. But he would do the hurting, too. He made most of it with black magic. Bad stuff. He make a root that could kill you dead, or kill someone you want dead. He could break up your marriage, or make your neighbor's cow get skinny and rot away while it's still alive. He was a powerful man, and he was called Dr. Shrike, 'cause a shrike is a bird that will nail something to a thorn to kill it before it eats it.

"One day a man comes looking for Dr. Shrike for a reason lots of men did. His woman was messing around on him. She was with lots of different men, all over the islands. Now normally Dr. Shrike would maybe make the woman sick, maybe give her burning inside, or maybe break her heart with a potion and make her never want to mess around again. But not this time.

"No one knows why this time was different. Maybe that man had a lot of money. Maybe that man was someone important. But Dr. Shrike did up a root that spread not just to one guilty man, but to all of them. Dr. Shrike could kill a man, I told you, but this time he killed fifty-two. No less than fifty-two men came down with the fever, and they died in their fields or their beds that very same day. Their bodies shriveled up where they fell, and their eyes turned blood red. Each one of them coughed up some bloody thing, like a little thing that might have been alive once. A piece of them. Every one of them died, but the woman lived.

"Fifty-two men were dead. Somebody's brother, somebody's cousin. Maybe their daddy or their granddaddy, even. If you weren't related to one of them, maybe he was your carpenter, or your bricklayer, or your field hand. Everyone on the islands knew one of them or more. Even the white folks. Wasn't a person didn't feel it when those men died, whether in their heart or in their wallets. Families fell apart. Businesses shut down. Whole villages were put into a dire way. They just stick huts out in the woods now, empty but for ghosts, maybe.

"People asked. People found out. It wasn't no secret who the most powerful root doctor on the islands was. They found out Dr. Shrike did it, but they couldn't do nothing about it. No way to prove it—and if there was, no one was brave enough to stand up to a man like that. Dr. Shrike got a new name, though. They called him by his real name, now, trying to take his power away. And they called him Sorry, for what he done to the people on those islands. Because of all the people he ever cursed and all the lives he ruined and all the evil he did. And people cursed him and hated him.

"Sorry George got old and no one ever got to him. People were too scared even when he was old—even other root doctors. He kept practicing until he was shriveled and old like I am now. I was just a boy when he died, but I knew of him. He died of natural causes, after all that. They buried him way out on one of them little islands where he was from. No one knows just where they put him, but lots of people think they know. It's like a riddle to find out where."

Dr. Crow paused. Minnow drew a long dry breath in through his nostrils.

"And now we come to where you come to my shack looking for help. And I got something I can help you with. I can get what you need easy, but I can't get what I need easy. I don't leave this place. I go to Bay Street when I need something. Everything else comes to me, just like you did. I'm safe right here. I can't be safe out there on them islands, where there's still strong magic and bad ghosts."

The candle flame drew long in the still air, a slender unmoving almond of yellow light.

"What do you need me to do?"

"This jar was full once," Dr. Crow said, picking up the little glass container, then setting it down again. "I need it full."

Minnow squinted, but the writing on the label was far too faded and the words were spidery and looped.

"If you want your daddy's medicine you gonna bring me goofer dust."

"Goofer dust?"

"Graveyard dust."

"Dust?" Minnow asked.

"From a grave."

"You don't mean from the church down the road."

Dr. Crow smiled again.

"No I do not. You gonna bring me dirt from Sorry George's grave, and I'll get you the medicine."

"You said no one knows where he's buried."

Dr. Crow shook his head.

"No one who is telling. But you may find someone if you look just right. Ain't no one like you ever tried to find it."

"Who can I look for?"

"Way out on them islands. You'll find someone."

"I don't even know where to start."

"First you got to get there. People live out there like there ain't no world across the river. I ain't seen them for years, but they may know."

"Is there a name? A place to look? I can't possibly find just one person on all those islands."

"You say you know Frogmore."

"I've been there."

"You find Auntie Mae out there and you tell her who you working for. Tell her what you looking for, and she'll help you if she can. She don't know nothing about Sorry George, but she can maybe find you someone who does."

"I can't do this."

"It ain't gonna be easy."

"How can I find something that you've never found?"

"It ain't gonna be easy. But if you want to try, it's there for you to try."

Dr. Crow reached behind his shoulder without looking and brought a small leather pouch down from the shelf and handed it to Minnow. The empty pouch could be cinched closed with a thread of leather woven through its top edge.

"You fill that up and bring it back to me, and our deal is done. Your daddy will live. I guarantee it."

Minnow wanted to leave. He thought of his father and took the pouch. He put it in his pocket and nodded.

"It doesn't sound so hard. It's just a trip across the river."

Dr. Crow didn't move. Then he turned his head left, right.

"You gonna have trouble."

"Pardon?"

"A man as bad as Sorry George ain't gonna let you get out there easy. He gonna make it hard."

"But he's dead."

Dr. Crow laughed.

"Death don't stop a hoodoo man. He's gonna try and stop you like he stopped everyone else who come before you."

"How?"

Dr. Crow tilted his head down, and his dark glasses lost the candlelight. The world outside fell silent, and the shack might have been buried under a mile of earth.

"Only he would know. But I know what I would do. And I can tell you that three things gonna come at you. It may be something you know, or someone you know. It may be a stranger, or something you never seen before. I don't know what, but it's gonna be three things. Some of them are already on their way. Some of them may be already here. But it's gonna be three things."

Minnow shook his head.

"What can I do?"

"Do what everybody does. Look for it, and when you see it, face it straight on. Ain't no use in running. Here."

Dr. Crow turned around and looked at the shelf. All Minnow could see was shadows and the edges of innumerable glass vials. Crow picked a flat flask with a cork in the top. It was smaller than a playing card.

"Don't you open this, till you need it most."

"What is it?"

"A potion that will help against evils. Old evils who respond to such things."

"Thank you."

Minnow put the vial inside the leather pouch. He put it back in his pocket, next to Varn's arrowhead, and when he looked up Dr. Crow was standing. Crow was tall, his head lost in the darkness. His dry voice sounded far away, like a ghost speaking from deep within an ancient crypt.

"There ain't nothing left for you to know or do here. You got to get on your way."

Minnow nodded and stood up.

"Don't come back here if you don't have what I want. Understand?"

"Yessir."

"Then go."

He backed out of the shack. Dr. Crow, invisible in the shadows, did not speak. Minnow closed the door and ran his finger along the blue trim. The river lapped at the muddy banks. A gull squawked. Men worked. The world outside went on.

He walked around the shack toward the docks. His stomach felt empty and sour after the secret meeting. He looked over the water at the dark line of the Island and its marsh apron spread on the other side of the wide river. Sorry George's final resting place would be even farther, over creeks and through woods and swamps and jungles. It was past lunchtime, and already his mother would be worried. He gazed back over Port Royal: dingy, muddy, bustling with workers and sailors. Back over the rooftops was the road to town, the road that would take him home. To his mother. To his father, still dying in bed. He'd return without the medicine and everything would be fine. His mother would understand. She'd be furious that he'd left town, and more furious that he'd gone all the way to Port Royal alone.

He walked along the shore past the docks, past a place where men hung big fish from hooks and scraped shiny scales. A man lay next to the workers, asleep or dead. He had no nose—just a black scabby hole—and yellow skin.

His mother would be upset that he'd come this far, but she didn't really have to know. Especially if he could get the medicine. If he had the medicine, maybe no one would ask anything but why the errand took so long. Maybe he was playing with his gang. Maybe he stopped to drink his soda and fell asleep in the sun. He had such a long way to go, though, to find the grave of a man he hadn't heard of until just moments before. A long way over the islands.

He heard laughing behind the fish cleaners. Boys his age. Two of them, one maybe younger, the other very close in age. They were maybe brothers: both had black curly hair, dirty white shirts, and cutoff pants. One held a rock in his hand, batting it against the side of a dog's head once, then twice. The dog—almost still a puppy—recoiled and pressed its back against the wooden wall, growling and then whimpering with closed eyes.

"Get him," the smaller boy said. He had pimples all over his face.

The bigger boy dropped the rock and lunged at the dog, putting two filthy hands around its neck. The dog shrieked and whipped its head to bite the boy, but could not reach. The younger boy kicked the animal in the stomach.

"Stop," Minnow said.

The little one kicked the dog again, and it wrenched in the older boy's hands.

"Stop that," Minnow said louder, and this time the bigger boy turned to see him. In that one instant the dog gained leverage and wrenched its neck free, snapping at the boy's hand but not biting him. The younger boy fell back, and the older boy stood up taller to avoid the dog's snapping. The dog lunged at him, then used the extra room to slip away around the side of the building.

"What'd you do that for?" the older boy said, stomping across the sand to Minnow's face. He was half a head taller and his breath smelled like onions.

"What did it do to you?" Minnow asked.

The older boy spit in his face, and as Minnow wiped the spit off, the older boy shoved both hands out into Minnow's chest and his breath went. He fell backward over the younger boy, on his hands and knees, and his lower back took the brunt of the fall against the hard-packed sand.

By the time he could scramble to his feet the boys were gone in the same direction as the dog.

Minnow brushed off his back and adjusted his short pants. He stood frozen, waiting for them to return. When they didn't, he started walking for the docks again, toward a busier part of the port. He watched over his shoulder as he went, but the boys were gone.

Then he smelled it: something salty and savory and good like the river itself. The warm aroma came in through his nostrils and made his chest ache. His stomach called for food.

Music floated to him from one of the nearest buildings: a continuous stream from an instrument that sounded like a high-pitched guitar. Something thumped along, giving deep rhythm to the song. He couldn't see inside, but he could smell smoke coming from the crooked pipe that vented the kitchen out to the plain, stinking world. A few men gathered at the door, smoking, and one man talked to a woman around the side. Another woman came walking from around back with a metal platter balanced on her palm.

"Five cents a hand," she called. "Five cents and fill your stomach."

Minnow approached slowly, watching the men, watching over his shoulder. The woman with the platter saw him and spun around once. Her long dress billowed out like a blooming flower. She leaned in and held the platter low.

"Five cents to fill your stomach, little boy."

The platter was arrayed with a circular pattern of boiled shrimp. Heads on, tails on, still in their dented shells, salted, glistening in the open air.

Minnow licked his lips and looked up at the woman.

"Five cents?" he asked.

She nodded.

He felt the billfold in his pocket and she watched him do it. His mother gave him the money for the medicine, and already half of it was gone with nothing to show. But he wouldn't need it now, if he completed his quest. Dr. Crow said to use it on the journey, and now it had begun. He had to start with something.

"Yes," he said, and took the quarter from the billfold. The lady held her hand out and he placed the quarter in her palm. She closed her palm and held the platter lower. He put out both hands to grab at the shrimp and she waved a finger.

"One hand. As much as you can hold, five cents."

He filled his dirty hand with shrimp: eight fat orange creatures damp and warm in his fingers. The lady flicked her wrist and two dimes appeared where the quarter had been. She gave them to him and went on her way, calling out her sale.

Minnow went to the water's edge and sat with the steaming shrimp in his lap. He picked the biggest one and shelled it, tossing the tail and head away. He ate the body whole, buttery and warm, dusted with red spice. He ate another, and another, and the dog returned.

It crept up behind him, close to the water, and sniffed the discarded shells. It plucked up a head and ate it whole, eyes and brain and long red whiskers. It leaned down again and ate a tail. The dog was not much more than a puppy: small, brown, covered in dirty curls from toes to tail. Two little black eyes showed through the thick mat of ringlets on its head. It had stunted puppy ears, floppy and short.

Minnow ate another shrimp and had four left. He shelled the next one and watched the dog lick the pebbles where the shrimp shells had been.

"Hello."

It stood alert: paws spread, legs straight, tail stiff. It sniffed the air. Minnow held out the shelled shrimp between two fingers and the dog stayed still.

"Come on."

It did not respond to his voice, but it moved when it was ready, stepping carefully across the sand to ease the shrimp from Minnow's fingers with the tips of its teeth. It gobbled it down, and Minnow threw the shells out for it too.

"I get the rest."

He ate the last three shrimp and tossed the shells and heads to the dog. He licked his fingers and wiped them on his stained pants.

"Good, huh?"

The dog perked up.

"Where you from?"

A raucous cheer came from some building in town. Men cheered and hollered, and a woman moaned and then screamed. Minnow's skin tightened on his arms, and the dog left, turning and trotting away toward the fish shacks.

Minnow stood up quick and brushed off his pants. There was plenty of day left, but he'd taken too long with his lunch. He checked his billfold and Dr. Crow's potion and looked up the beach toward the docks. A ferry or a barge would be leaving for the Island. He just had to find it.

He left his lunch spot and passed the fish shacks. No dog, and no boys either. He craned his neck as he approached the tangle of wooden docks along the river's edge, looking for someone about to leave.

All was work and activity. Men loaded boats. The sailors were big, muscled, burned brown. Most wore no shirts, and many were crossed with scars or places where fresh cuts had healed pink. A few were in departure, casting their bowlines off and pushing away from the salt-crusted docks. He watched some of them begin their course across the water. He tapped his thigh with his hand. He'd never been to the Island alone. He'd never crossed the river alone.

A bell rang out at the end of the longest dock. He passed several shorter piers, walking over their ramps as he went by. Most of the boats out on the water were small, but the biggest were the shrimp boats. Maybe a ferry would come down from Charleston or up from Savannah and dwarf them, but now the kings of the port were the long shrimp-ing skiffs arrayed with many nets. Their captains would be hard men, men who worked under the sun for days as their nets trawled deep waters.

The smell of salty, muddy barnacles hit the back of his throat. Minnow licked his lips and tasted the shrimp again. He crossed another dock and looked down its length. It wasn't quite as crowded, and it moored no shrimp boats. Instead he saw smaller bateaux meant to carry people to and from larger boats anchored out in the bay. A few barges were there, and one at the end appeared to be empty.

He looked up and down the shore again, checked over his shoulder, and stepped onto the ramp. It stayed low to the sand, and then low to the water until it went upward to avoid the cycling tide. The water was midway and dropping now, the shore showing more mud and muddy oysters and mud-slick flotsam. Clumps of barnacles growing on the pil-ings perfumed the salty air.

He walked carefully. The dock was not for rich couples on Bay Street or for vacationers down from the north. This was a work dock, with thin bowing planks laid just close enough to walk on. Big gaps showed gray-green water below. Garfish the size of hogs surfaced in the shadows and sucked at the surface for algae and brine.

He passed the first small craft, and then another. A sailor sat in one, hat slung low, napping. The next few were empty, but one dinghy had a negro in it repairing a sail. Minnow went on, and then stopped to look back at the shore, feet split between two different boards. The dock shivered under him in the wind and the current, just enough to feel. The port behind bustled with people and animals and carts. Dr. Crow's shack stood like a dark monolith down on the oyster rake, and at the end of the dock stood the three men he'd run across when he had arrived at the port. They saw him, and they were coming, and they knew he was trying to leave.

Minnow turned quick and looked down the length of the dock. Only a few more boats, all of them empty, and then a barge tied all the way out at the head. A negro sat in it with a long pole laid over his lap. Minnow sped up, stepping fast over gapped boards, then skipping one, two. He glanced over his shoulder, and the men were coming down the dock, single file, cigar smoker in lead.

He was almost there. He threw up a hand in a half wave, half salute. The negro in the barge was old, older than Dr. Crow, wearing a floppy straw hat. He looked up and the hat tilted back.

"Will you take me to the Island?" Minnow asked, chest heaving, almost going straight into the barge. He stopped himself short on the edge of the dock and caught his balance.

"The Island? I'm waiting on a load. I'll take you then."

"I'm in a hurry, and I can pay."

"How much you paying?"

"I have twenty cents," he lied.

"I don't need twenty cents to row you to the Island. Your daddy know you got that money?"

Minnow looked over his shoulder. The men were coming faster. One of them had a hand up and cigar man was yelling something.

"Yessir. I just need a ride really fast."

The negro took the pole off his lap and stood up.

"They coming with you?"

"No sir."

The old negro laughed and plunged the pole into the river and pushed off.

"Then untie that rope fast before I pull the dock down."

Minnow knelt down and unwound the thick, frayed bow-line. He tossed it in, jumped, cleared the watery gap, and rolled flat onto his back. The three men were passing the last boat on the dock now, waving their hands. Yelling. Cursing. The negro raised his hand high and called out.

"I'll be back in just a while. Don't worry."

Minnow looked up at him.

"Thank you."

The negro turned and gave one last push with the pole before the water was too deep for it.

"They just drunk or something. Probably got a bad idea. They'll forget about you before you set foot on the mud over there."

Minnow nodded, rolled off his back and moved up onto his haunches, fingertips down on the rough planks to steady himself against the gentle rocking of the river.

The old negro took a long oar and began to paddle on the left, the right, guiding them away from shore. The tide flowed out to the east, starboard, as it emptied to a low tide. A steady breeze blew over them, blowing Minnow's hair and cooling his body. The river was busy, but other craft made way for the barge as it glided across. The river was wide, and even with the skilled paddling they had only just reached the midway point. The captain made great swooping strokes, each one propelling the craft as if two men were at the oar.

"I drop at only one spot," the captain said.

"Any spot is fine with me. Just on the Island."

"Where you going?"

"Frogmore."

"Frogmore?"

"Yessir."

"That's a long way out. You know someone there?"

"Auntie Mae. I'm looking for her."

"I don't know Auntie Mae."

"I'll find her."

He checked his belongings and looked back to watch Port Royal grow smaller against the shore. He looked ahead and the Island loomed, just trees in the direction they were headed. Water lapped at the edges of the barge.

"Stand up and look. Don't be scared."

Minnow stood up and watched the Island grow larger before him. It stretched across his view as far as he could see: broad fields of marsh spreading out before the dark band of trees. The marsh buffered the land from the river, unlike at the port, and the captain steered them toward one of a thousand dark cuts in the lush summer grass. Way down the curving river, to port, Minnow could see the white line of buildings on Bay Street. The Episcopal steeple glinted in the sun, a slender gray peak that marked his distant neighborhood.

The captain moved faster now, waltzing left and right to paddle the water and steer the blocky craft into the creek. Little buildings showed themselves in the tree line: houses maybe, a little store perhaps. The barge slipped into the mouth of a creek. The grass was tall, up to Minnow's shoulders even when standing. It grew in patches that blended together into low forests of green. Birds lighted from place to place, fishing and resting in the hidden greens. A big fiddler waved a claw at Minnow from its perch on a thin green shoot, and then watched the barge float on. The creek narrowed and the captain kept them true, with the marsh even on both sides. Sometimes when the sides brushed the edge of the marsh, periwinkles dropped from the blades of the marsh grass and tapped against the salted wood like pebbles.

The captain put the oar down and took up the long pole. The end was gray with sulfurous pluff mud. He stuck it back in and guided the craft along, sometimes lifting it up and swinging it across the front of the barge to push the other side.

"Here we go," the captain said to the water as he eased deeper into the marsh.

They passed the remnants of a dock. The pilings stood crooked and coated with barnacles. A few sea roaches scurried around the pilings to hide from view. The creek tightened around them and the barge seemed to glide over the marsh itself, and then they began to emerge. Marsh gnats swarmed Minnow's face.

"We close. You gonna throw the rope."

Minnow nodded. A marsh hen cackled and the creek let them go. He could see the muddy bottom now as they glided into shallow water before the shore. There was only one dock there, pointed out toward them, with a few negroes working nearby. When Calico had brought Minnow and his father over, they had docked at a place almost as busy as Port Royal, where the main road led through the Island to Frogmore. This was a quiet place, empty but for the handful of negroes and the one barge gliding noiselessly up to the dock.

"Throw the rope."

Minnow took the coil and flung it out to the head of the dock where a colored boy caught it and pulled the barge up. It bumped the dock and the boy tied it off and went about his business.

"Good. Now you jump. And don't run off."

"No sir."

Minnow waited for the barge to ease toward the dock and jumped the gap to the head. The old negro set his pole down and eased himself up like a creaking skeleton. He came across onto the dock and Minnow helped him with his hand. The man's hand was calloused and hard, like a turtle's shell.

"Thank you, son."

Minnow nodded and took the billfold out so the man would know he meant to pay. He took out two dimes and held them close to his body, looking at them in his palm.

"One of those is enough, son. You keep the other one for where you're going."

Minnow examined the silver coins. He'd need to eat again at dinner, and maybe he would need money to get back. He put one dime in the fold without showing the other quarter, and handed the second dime to the old man.

"Thank you, son."

"Thank you for the ride, sir."

The old man smiled.

"Everyone calls me Charlie. You get to needing a ride back and can't find one, follow this road up here and see if I'm around. I'll take you for free."

"Thank you."

The old negro reached out and set his hand on the top of Minnow's head.

"You be careful out there. It ain't like town."

"I know, sir."

"You don't."

Minnow left the dock and walked across the landing. Pine trees surrounded the spot, which was no more than a small pine-needle clearing carved out of the woods on a sliver of the Island's southern face. There was the dock and a few shacks and one building that might have been a store. A few goats grazed in a grassy patch on one side of the clearing, and a group of children played near them. A single cart rolled northward, away from the clearing, down the narrow forest road.

He took the road out, into the trees away from the rough clearing. The cart ahead of him picked up its pace and then was gone around a bend. The clopping faded through the trees, the noise from the landing fell away, and the woods were quiet.

Minnow looked over his shoulder and then over his head. The canopy of pines and water oaks came together into a shadowed web, like interlocking fingers blocking the falling sun. He walked the light-dappled path down the center, and no one else came along to move him. The world was quiet and dim.

His mother would certainly be looking for him, by now. She might not leave the house, but maybe someone from his gang came by, and she'd have them looking. He'd gotten lost before, gotten in trouble, gotten stuck someplace or another. She would be afraid, especially because of the money, but she knew he would be fast. He would not leave the path.

He didn't know where the cart road would go, but he could look for the bigger route that ran north to Frogmore—the road he and his father had once traveled together. That road would have people on it, unlike the deserted forest path, and maybe a place where he could get some water. He licked his lips.

Minnow walked the road and passed only one old gray lady with a basket in her arms. She kept her head low and did not look at him. He did not speak to her, either, and the two went on in separate directions. Once or twice he heard something tramping through the woods, bigger than a squirrel. He checked for anything or anyone that might be following, thought of Sorry George, and continued on without further sign of any living thing.

The slender oaks gave way to stunted pine saplings that had grown beneath the shadow of their larger ancestors. Then a field of saw palmettos engulfed the forest floor and strangled the saplings, spreading out into a solid underbrush of emerald fans broken only by tall, mature pine trunks. The sun fell ever farther, and the high-needled canopy made the world below look dim. He followed the narrowing road between two shoulder-high walls of spiked palm fronds. Now and then one would brush him as he passed, and that soft whisper was the only sound in the woods.

※

THE SAW PALMETTOS RELENTED and the choked road widened into a proper path for wagons and people alike. A ditch
ran down one side, and the way was heavily trodden. The
canopy broke and allowed ruby light down to the road. He
passed a few people on foot, but they turned down a side
path into the forest and disappeared. No one overtook him,
even as the road broadened before the main avenue.

He found his road, the big one that ran up the Island.
South would take him to docks and the place where Calico
launched as he ferried between the Island and Bay Street.
North would lead to Frogmore and the heart of the Island.
He could see water off across the road, through the trees:
one of the main river's many wide branches.

The road ran busy with people and carts. Most of the loads
were crops, food, or building supplies. Mostly negroes were
on the path, except for the occasional white person visiting
from town. Even the men driving the carts and leading the
oxen were colored. A crowd of workers, sailors—more of
them white than anyone—and women went up and down
the road, mixed with the carts and wagons.

Negro women sat lined on the side of the road in the
shade of tall palmettos. They wove baskets out of long, thin
bands of sweetgrass, yellow and green. They wove patterns
carried over from where their grandparents and great-grand-
parents had come from. They wove circles and spirals that
had never been told of on a piece of paper. Minnow stopped
to study the baskets, and the women smiled and spoke
and clucked to each other at his presence. He watched one
woman work on an unfinished piece: slender brown fingers
wove the dampened flat reeds into a tight coil that formed
a long basket shape with a wide bottom. The weaver looked
up and smiled, and Minnow smiled back.

The road went through more woods, away from the southern part of the Island. Frogmore peeked through the trees ahead and then came up to meet him as the path emerged again from the trees. Two rows of low buildings lined the path left and right, forming the heart of Frogmore. The town stretched out behind that into a sprawling mix of houses and stores and barns and fields. Somewhere beyond that were wild woods and swamps.

Minnow glanced from face to face. Dark faces, women, children, men. Most garbed in light island wear: blousy white pants, sandals, men with no shirts at all. Some were locals, some sailors as always, and travelers passing south to Newport. He searched for someone who might know Auntie Mae or be friendly enough to at least take his question seriously. He approached the buildings and decided against asking someone on the road. A shopkeeper would be different, maybe.

A dozen buildings stood in the downtown row. One was an inn, seemingly empty; and a honky-tonk was open to the road and packed with guests who drank and laughed and ate. He passed a general store and a store that sold furniture crafted from raw wood. Many of the doors were painted blue, as was the trim around the windows and shutters. He got to the end and turned back to reconsider the stores. The breeze blew, and a note rang out next to him.

On the other side of the road, and up a little, was a wrought-iron pole with many arms, stuck in the ground. It stood as tall as Minnow, and a glass bottle adorned each arm. The colors were red and blue and brown and clear. The breeze blew and the bottles hummed a low, ghostly song. A little shack stood up a gravel walk from the bottles. The door was open and a small window was open, too. The trim on both was painted blue.

A small negro boy came out of the door and stopped when he saw Minnow. He was younger than Minnow by a few years, but almost as tall. He came on down after a pause and stopped by the bottle tree.

"Who're you?"

"I'm looking for someone."

"Who're you looking for?" the boy stuck out one hand as if to take payment but then waved it up into the air. He wore knee-length short pants and suspenders, but his chest was bare and shiny with sweat.

"Someone named Auntie Mae."

"Don't know her."

"He's right," a new voice said. This one was behind Minnow. A deep voice. He turned to see a huge woman standing where the walk met the road. All three stood there under the sun, lined up on the path. The sun had dropped low to the horizon and now cast the world in harsh angled light.

"I'm sorry," Minnow said, and started moving away from the boy, angling away from the big woman.

"Don't be. Why you looking?" the woman asked. She wore a long white dress that ballooned out over her hips.

"Just looking," Minnow said.

"She used to live near here. Who sent you to her? Whoever it is ain't been out here in a long time," she said. She walked up the path toward the boy and the bottles, passing Minnow and stopping at the boy.

"She moved out. Way out on the islands. Live with people out there, now. Ain't none of them ever come to Frogmore. Not much, at least."

She put her hand on the boy's shoulder, and Minnow nodded.

"Thank you. Sorry to bother you."

"Don't you want to know where they are?"

He'd just wanted to go, to get away, but now he nodded.

"You take the road on out. You ever been out there?"

Minnow shook his head.

"Well, not much is out there. The road gonna get smaller, then you gonna be in the woods if you follow it long enough. Most people never take it that far, but that's your way. Why you out here alone? Where your daddy?"

"Sick, ma'am."

"When you in the woods, cross the river you come to. That's the island they on, up around the side where you won't see 'em at first. But head straight out on the road. You go left or right too much and you wind up crossin' to the wrong island."

The breeze fluted through the bottles and a few of them shifted and clinked against the metal arms.

"Thank you, ma'am."

"You welcome. Be careful in them woods. And get your dog off my grass before he wets it."

Minnow turned and spoke at the same time.

"I don't have a—"

The little brown dog sat on its rump at the edge of the grass, hind legs tucked, forelegs straight up and down.

"—dog."

He turned back to the shack, and they were just closing the door to him. He looked back and the dog was there, snapping at a fly.

Minnow crossed the grass and stopped, and held his hand out to the dog, who didn't regard it at all. Minnow put his hand on top of the dog's curly head and patted it a few times. The dog looked around the yard and the road, and then up at Minnow.

"You coming?"

Minnow set off away from the buildings, farther up the road and into the Island. The dog sat on the edge of the grass, uncaring, and then scampered along to catch up with him. Minnow nodded and kept walking.

HE LEFT THE LAST buildings of Frogmore as the sun's lower edge fell below the tree line behind him. The woman's advice would take him farther out. Maybe too far, if it really meant crossing to another island. Leaving the Island had not been in the plan. It had Frogmore, plantations, villages, and people, all connected by well-traveled roads. But the chain of islands that led out toward the wild ocean was an entirely different matter.

The sun would be hidden in the trees soon, and darkness was not far away. The long summer day would linger, but it would end, the moon would rise, and he'd never spent a night outside of Newfort in his life. He quickened his pace, and the dog did too. He thought maybe he could make it to Auntie Mae, finish his business, and return to Frogmore before nightfall. If he could get back to Frogmore before dark, little would keep him from getting all the way into town. If something went wrong, he'd have to brave it overnight. He could hide out somewhere for the night, if he had to. Find a shed, or some abandoned barn. He and the gang did that sort of thing all the time, back home.

"Let's get going," he said, and broke into a trot.

The dog obliged, and came nipping at his heels as if to speed them along.

The road narrowed, and the slight traffic coming and going from Frogmore thinned and then disappeared, with one final oxcart passing them. The sun did not relent on its fast decline, and soon just a band of reddened sky was visible where the road left a clear place in the trees. The woods tightened their grip with each step, and soon the road began to fade.

Minnow slowed and tried to catch his breath. He glanced over his shoulder and nodded at the pink sunset, then turned ahead again. Compared to the lighter sky behind him, the road ahead seemed gray and green and shadowy. They went on, and he and the dog walked the right rut of a two-rut path, with tall grass growing down the middle. The surrounding forest was more a jungle now: tight with pines and saw palmettos, tangled with twisted vines and moss. The world smelled damp, and cool, and dark. He smelled salt, too, and thought of the river he sought. But the whole island smelled like salt when the breeze blew.

The sun set far below the trees, but still a dim light kept the sky gray and held back the stars and the light of the rising moon. The false day hung overhead, and Minnow pushed on down the road with the dog at his side.

They went even faster, covered a long stretch of road, and dusk turned the world dim. His legs ached, and he looked left and right into the trees as the jungle turned black. He'd been out at night alone a few times in the woods near town, but not in the creeping, tangled wild of the Island.

He kept his pace. The deepest parts of the woods fell black as pitch, and crickets began a high rhythmic note that seemed to fill the whole world. The dog came closer to him, and he put his hand on its matted curls. The divot of sky over his head faded from gray to purple to black, and the road was only a faint cut in the silver grass. He looked over his shoulder again and saw a black maw between the trees, and ahead the same: a blank black portal through the trees. The cricket-song rose in crescendo, and then fell again like the rhythmic sound of the ocean.

Minnow stumbled and then fell to his knees, scrambling away from the middle of the road to sit in the shadows. The dog stayed in the faint column of moonlight at the center of the path. Minnow put a hand on his trembling knees. Nothing. Nothing around but the dog, and that was good. He listened, watched, and nodded at the empty shadows.

"Come here," he whispered, and the dog came. "Sit down."

The dog sat next to him and he put his hand on its back. His legs calmed. A toad croaked a guttural passage deep in the woods behind them and then stopped. He looked back down the road as far as he could see in the dark. Frogmore back that way, and the road to the little ferry that had brought him. No. Not a free ride into Port Royal. He could pay Calico to take him to town and he'd be home, safe. His mother would be relieved and his father, who was probably dying, wouldn't know the difference.

The dog licked its forepaw and then considered him.

"What?"

Minnow looked up the path and could see the trees and brush closing in even tighter.

"It's right up there. The river. And Auntie Mae. Maybe we can stay the night with her."

The crickets stopped and he stood up, looking over his shoulder into the woods. Anything would be better than those woods.

He patted the dog on the head and started up the path again. Then it ended. He stopped and looked at the wall of trees before him, and he wanted to cry. Where had this road led him, but to the end of all ways? He'd passed dozens of side roads and paths along the way: some just black holes in the dark woods. Where had they gone off to?

He pushed on through tall weeds and then entered the forest itself, dark and green and shiny in the humid night. He stopped now and then to listen for sounds of the river. It would not be flowing like a freshwater river, but it might rustle in its marshy banks or bring the sounds of marsh hens or splashing rays. But he heard nothing.

He pressed on through the forest. The dog ranged away from him, sniffing stumps, chasing things in the underbrush, and then leaving his sight entirely. The forest closed in and he pushed through knee-high saw palmettos tangled with vines. He thought about snakes and raccoons and bugs the size of his palm. The pine trees grew tall to block out the moonlight, and when he looked up he saw nothing but darkness.

A dog howled. He looked around and couldn't see the one that had followed him, but now he wished it was back. He saw no sign of it, so he focused on his steps and kept on, keeping his straight line by moving from tree to tree. He could smell the salt. Surely the river was near. She had said it was near.

He picked up a game trail and stopped for a moment, kneeling down to touch the flattened grass and leaves. He looked along the narrow corridor cut between the low pal-metto fronds. Boars, maybe. Deer. Raccoon, possum. He wished for the dog again but did not hear or see it at all. The way directly ahead was thick with fronds and dotted with broad-trunked pine trees. The game knew the way, and they cut the easiest path. Maybe they'd be trying to get to the same place he was.

He stood up and looked over the sea of palm fronds. He followed the path, listening for other early evening travelers.

The trail led away from his original route but then bent east again. The animals might make stops along the river. The path would take him there, but something might be down there feeding or hiding in the mud. Alligators didn't live in salt water, but they lived near it. On banks, even. He thought about Sorry George. The three things that would come his way. Crow had warned him.

The woods were quiet, crickets silent.

The fronds on his right exploded with movement, and out came the dog, bounding onto the game trail. It went sniffing off ahead of him, nose to the pine straw.

"You go ahead."

He followed the dog along the trail and it did not come to the river. He couldn't tell how far they'd gone in all the trees, but when the path bent to the right again he was deep into the night. He sat down and buried his face in his hands. It was getting late. His legs hurt. His eyes ached from straining in the dark world. Most of all he regretted taking the trail. He looked up from his dirty palms and thought of cutting straight east again, but he wasn't sure where east was in all the trees, and he couldn't have broken through the frond walls anyway.

He was about to stand up and head back down the trail to where he first got on it—if he could tell—when he saw the dog was standing alert, pointing like a hound on the scent. Then Minnow caught it too, coming in on a cool evening breeze that moved the fronds and hushed the forest. Smoke. He moved up to one knee and thought about calling to the dog but then didn't. He made a low hissing sound and the dog didn't move.

Minnow waddled forward, still on his haunches, and crouched next to the dog. The forest appeared gray to his night eyes. When he came around a bend, he saw the light that had caught the dog's attention, and the source of the smoke, and the men with guns.

Maybe the trail was for game. Maybe the men just used it to get to their camp, or maybe they made the trail themselves to look like animals had done it. Two men were there: one on his knees, feeding logs into a roaring fire, and the other standing at the edge of the clearing, hidden in shadows. The man at the fire had a big pistol tucked in his belt, and the shadow man cradled some long firearm in his arms. From where he stood he'd be the one to see Minnow first.

Minnow backed up around the bend and pulled the dog with him, hoping the movement would escape any eyes. The fire was bright. Everything around the clearing would be like the bottom of the ocean.

Soft steps fell behind him, padding down the leafy trail. Someone was coming up the path, but he had nowhere to go except into the clearing or back toward the footsteps. He could not now try the sharp, dark mass of fronds that surrounded him. A light drew close, and then it was on him, and then the shadow.

"What the hell?"

The man held a dripping torch out in front, high over his head, and the orange light cast its glow over Minnow and the dog and the whole path. The dog turned on the torch-bearer, snarled its lip, and then darted into the underbrush. It had no trouble with the fronds, and Minnow watched him go. He looked up at the man from his position on his back, propped up on his hands.

"What the hell are you doing out here?"

The man came in on him, swinging the torch in an arc over his head. His next words were a muted call, like he was yelling, but trying to be quiet.

"We got something here!"

Noise came from the clearing, and then another man came up behind Minnow, looking down at him on the ground. He had the long gun in his arms.

"What's that?"

"Just found him here on the trail."

"On the trail?"

"Yup."

"You spying on us? You with the police?" The man leaned in and his face was a skeleton's shadow.

"No, sir. I'm lost."

"Lost?"

"Yessir."

"Out here?"

"Yessir."

"You reckon he's telling the truth?" the torchbearer asked. The other man stood up taller.

"Was that your dog I saw run out that way?"

Minnow nodded. "Sort of."

"What do you mean?"

"He's been following me for a while."

"Anyone else following you?"

"No, sir. I came up from Frogmore looking for the river. I'm looking for a village out across it."

"With negroes?"

Minnow nodded. "I think, sir."

"I don't know no village up there," the torchbearer offered.

"If you just point me to the river, I'll be gone."

"What you going to do at the river?"

"Cross it."

The torchbearer laughed.

"You ain't got a boat."

Minnow tried to speak, but the torchbearer cut him off.

"Let's take him up the path. Get him to the fire."

Minnow looked into the foliage, at the little break in the fronds that the dog had escaped into. The shadow man noticed.

"No, no. Don't want to get caught like a coon, do you?"

Minnow shook his head.

"What do we do to coons?" the torchbearer asked, his flame dripping on the path, hissing and sputtering. Minnow didn't move.

"We skin 'em. And we eat 'em," he said. "Now get up."

Minnow rose to his feet and dusted off his hands. He tried to keep them steady, though his heart rattled in his chest and a cold sweat formed on his back. He tried to see their faces, tried to tell how old they were.

"Come on."

They took him up the trail and around the corner, calling a warning as they did.

"It's us. Us and one more. Look out."

Shadow man led the way after torchbearer called out their arrival. They entered the clearing and a third man, who fed the fire, moved out of the shadows with his pistol drawn.

"Who's the boy?"

"Put the damn gun down, Jack."

"Who's the boy?"

"We just found him on the trail."

"On the trail?"

"Right back there."

"Spying?"

"We ain't sure," torchbearer said and gave Minnow a little push farther into the clearing. Minnow looked around at the shadow edge of the clearing. The trees and bushes moved in the breeze. A river breeze. He smelled salt, strong on the air, and heard marsh whispers.

The fire dominated the clearing, with a few cut stumps placed around for stools. A metal-strapped trunk sat at one dark edge. Jack, the man with the pistol, kept glancing at the trunk.

"What you here for? You got police with you?" shadow man asked.

Minnow shook his head.

"You don't talk much," Jack said. "You better get talking."

"Sit him by the fire," shadow man said, and torchbearer pushed him ahead. He put his free hand on Minnow's shoulder and pressed down until Minnow was sitting cross-legged before the campfire. Torchbearer stuck his flaming brand into the ground away from the blaze. "Maybe he'll talk more."

In the fire he could see them all better: Jack, skinny, pistol in hand. Shadow man with his rifle, skinny too, hollow eyes, bony body. The torchbearer was the big one.

"I just want to get to the river," Minnow said.

"You didn't quite make it, did you?" torchbearer asked.

Minnow shook his head.

"What ought we do with you? I think you might be looking for someone. Looking for us. We can't let you go," shadow man said, picking at a tooth with one long fingernail.

"I'm here alone. I'm looking for someone named Auntie Mae in a village on the other side of the river."

"I don't know," shadow man said. "Maybe we should throw him in the fire and see how he cooks."

Minnow stared at the fire.

"No sir."

Torchbearer laughed and shadow man grinned broadly.

"Maybe we ought to take him to the river after all. Put him in and see how he swims out there in the dark," shadow man said. "You hear how big them sharks get out in the sound? Eat a bateau whole."

Minnow looked around the clearing for any way out. The game trail led back. At the head of the clearing, in the shadows, he saw another way out. Maybe toward the river.

"Or maybe we should just have some fun with him ourselves," Jack said in a low voice.

Torchbearer touched his chin and nodded.

"If he's going out there to the negroes we might as well stop him right here. Knowing what they might do," Jack whispered.

"You know what they might do?" shadow man asked, pacing around the fire to check the blaze, then stopping again to look down on Minnow.

"I'm looking for help from them. To find someone. Something," Minnow said, trying to find the right words fast.

"They gonna eat you," Jack hissed.

"Yup," shadow man said. "Deputy went out there just last month to calm them folks down. Never came back till the tide brought his body in. All covered in tooth holes." Shadow man clapped loud when he said *tooth*. Torchbearer laughed, but Jack held up his hand.

"Y'all get quiet, 'specially if he got someone with him."

"I'm alone," Minnow said.

"We know you is," Jack said and walked over to the big trunk. He put his gun on top of it and reached down to his pants to adjust his belt.

"You got anything we should know about?" torchbearer asked.

Minnow thought of his potion and his billfold, and the few coins he had left. His hand stayed still. He shook his head.

"You got nothing but a wild dog to follow you?" torchbearer asked and reached one giant callused hand down to Minnow's face.

The game trail exploded with movement, noise, cries, barking. Jack whipped around with his pistol in hand and fired. Sparks and smoke sprayed across the clearing. Someone screamed and then all three men were yelling at once. Someone dove across the clearing and tackled shadow man, the smallest one, and torchbearer went diving into the darkness. Minnow scrambled up to all fours and started for the dark cut at the top of the clearing. Someone tripped over him and stuck a boot in his ribs. The wind left him and he sprawled on his back long enough to see someone on top of torchbearer, strangling him.

"I told you!" Jack yelled over and over, shooting his gun again and again. He looked right at Minnow but did not seem to notice him in the shadows. Minnow sucked in a hard breath and slid out into the darkness.

Another shadow came blasting out from the game trail, and it was the last thing Minnow saw of the glowing clearing. He jumped to his feet and ran as fast as he could into the darkness, struggling through vine-twisted limbs. Pine branches swatted his face, and low saw palmetto fronds stabbed at his legs. He glanced back once but saw only shadows and trees and long braids of moss hanging from limbs like long beards.

Someone ran right by but didn't see him. Whoever it was turned off the path and went deep into the woods. Minnow pushed on, smelling the salt air, feeling the ground go soft under his feet. The trees became sparse and the brush pulled away and tall clumps of marsh grass grew from the loamy earth. The next few steps took him onto even softer ground, and then the mud sucked at his shoes and threatened to strip them off.

He high-stepped across the mud but soon it was too soft for motion. He sank up to his ankles, and only through some miracle was he able to keep his shoes. He tipped forward and knew he'd soon be face down in the slimy gray mud, but instead he landed on something hard. He put his palms down on rough planks and pulled himself up onto a wooden platform, freeing his feet from the mud. The platform rocked, and he realized he was on a flat barge at the water's edge. The river. He looked back again and saw no one. He scrambled to the back of the barge, stayed on his stomach, and plunged his hands down into shallow water and mud. He pushed off. He pushed off hard and extended his arms, and the barge

slipped free. He searched for a rope or a line and found nothing. The platform spun once, and then floated free of the
mud and marsh and out into the river.

He rolled over onto his back and watched the dark shore-
line of the Island disappear. He'd never left it, never been out
farther than that bit of land. He saw no sign of the clearing
behind him, no fire or people moving at all. He turned over
and scanned the dark water: gray and black and churning all
around, licking up onto the edge of the raft. But the craft
was dry and floating fine, except for the spray. He peered out
into the darkness ahead and could not see the other side of
the river, or any land beyond. For just a moment his heart
stopped, and he thought he might have pushed out into the
open ocean, but he couldn't remember any real surf where
he'd left the land. He had to be on a river, but it was wide,
dark, and endless.

He tried to move up on the raft to balance it out, but it
tipped forward and almost sent him sliding into the black
water. He was as strong a swimmer as any boy raised in
Newfort, but he swam in gentle creeks and at the edge of
rivers—not the churning black water that rocked his raft
now. He gazed out over the water and saw whitecaps breaking the black surface. Chop in the water: from waves, or
made by some creature from the depths—some leviathan
risen from the river-bottom. He couldn't tell.

The wind picked up and blew down the river's course,
over the raft, sending it spinning and then careening across
the black. Salt water sprayed over him and put salty drops
on his lips. The wind howled, and the raft tilted again. He
cried out.

He flattened and lifted his chin enough to see out over
the river. A low, dark line stretched across his view, and he

entered sparse marsh grass and then a thicker field. The dark line rose into the shape of trees. The water was calmer in the marsh, and he scooted to one side to paddle the raft toward land. The wind was with him, or he would have been pushed back out to the river. With the wind and the tide aiding him, he pushed far into the marsh and could barely see a high bluff, pale in the night.

The raft turned again. He paddled and splashed, and in some places he could hit mud with his hands and push off. The bluff rose before him, and the raft ran aground. He got to his feet, jumped, landing in the twisted roots that tangled the side of the sandy, muddy bluff.

He kicked the raft away, sending it out into the shallow water where it began to drift away with the wind. It might be useful later, but it would also be easy to see once the sun came up. Anyone would be able to tell where he had come to shore. He didn't know who'd raided the camp, but either of the involved parties might be interested in him. He watched the raft go and nodded his head.

He heaved his breath in and out against the thick, swampy air. He hunkered down there catching his breath, moving his hands over his head, face, body, hips. He hadn't lost anything. He wasn't hurt. He looked across the river and could see the faintest flicker of orange through the trees. The wind brushed away any sound that might have been coming from that side. Minnow put his arms around his knees and tried to stop from shivering. He'd left the Island, and he was alone.

Minnow looked up the bluff, up the sandy slope to the white edge cut against the black sky. He used twisted roots as handholds to struggle up the muddy base, then scrambled up the sandy side to the top. He tumbled over the peak and down the other side into a light beach forest. A plume of white dust rolled down with him into the shadows.

He'd hoped to find shacks, or sheds, or animals, or any sign of a village. He'd hoped that maybe he'd found Auntie Mae without even trying. Instead he saw only low saw palmettos mixed under thin gray water oaks. The ground was

light and sandy, leading away to where the island was dark
with thick jungle.

Minnow slid down the rest of the way to the bottom of
the bluff and heard barking. He glanced over his shoulder
and saw nothing, nothing, just like the missing village. No
people. No Auntie Mae. Maybe Sorry George, though.
He was out there somewhere, coming for Minnow just as
Minnow was coming for him.

He looked back down and a shape stood in the bushes.
It broke through the nearest ragged edge of brush: the dog,
sniffing the ground as it trotted into the open. It stopped,
sniffed the air, and turned its nose to Minnow.

"How'd you get across?"

The dog puffed out its sides and sighed.

"You're not running from someone, are you?"

The dog didn't respond. Minnow gazed out into the dark
woods.

"What now?"

He was wet. His pants were wet from sloshing around
on the raft. His shirt was damp from the spray. His hair
was slick with sweat, and his body trembled as a cool night
breeze blew over the bluff. The dog shook his body and came
closer to him, but not close enough to offer any warmth.

"I don't have anything for a fire. Someone in the village
might. Anyone out here might."

He paused at the last words, considering who else might
be out on a barrier island that late at night. People lived out
on the islands. Big islands were arrayed with entire plantations. Smaller islands had no more than a mound of bluff
and some sea oats clinging on top. The one he'd found could
be the smallest, or the largest. For now, he could see only the
bluff behind him and the woods ahead.

"What do you think?"

The dog went down and stretched on the ground, resting its head between two paws.

"We can't stop tonight. We're too close to that camp. We need to keep going."

The moon had risen high, but it was only a yellow sliver in the clearing over his head. Minnow heaved in a deep breath and thought about Bay Street, and his father back home, and his mother probably sitting up awake. Candles would be burning in their room, waiting on a son who'd disappeared without a warning. He felt as if a year had passed since he'd left Bay Street, just going on a short trip. Now he was backed up against a sandy dune, staring into darkness. His eyelids fell low, and his stomach yearned for a dinner he hadn't had and probably would not have.

No road, no path: just thin, skeleton trees clacking their branches where they grew close together. Moss hung from their limbs in long tendrils that drifted to and fro in the river breeze.

An owl hooted, and the dog sat up, ears perked.

Something ran across the blackness in front of him: a darker shape through the shadowy gray. At first he thought it was a man, maybe from the camp, maybe following the dog over the river. But it moved too fast, flying across his vision, landing only the lightest footfalls on the soft ground. And it wasn't an animal. The shape was surely something on two legs.

The owl hooted as if in warning: deep, deeper than should have been possible.

"We need to go."

He brushed his palms off and stood up, adjusting his clothes and checking his meager possessions. The owl took flight, revealing its high perch in a spindly oak. The branch swung as the owl pushed off and spread dark wings against the night. It flew off like a winged demon that might have been spying on them, or hunting them as game.

"Let's go."

Minnow started off into the woods, not sure of his path, just hoping to find a sign of life that might be friendly to a boy and a dog late at night.

He entered the first few trees and the moon gave faint silver light to his path. The way seemed clear enough. He picked up his pace, and then he hit the web. It felt thick, like damp yarn tied between the trees. He bounced back and then tore the sticky web from his face and his cheeks. His hand dropped on something warm, soft, bulbous. The spider bit him on the temple, a quick sting, and scurried to escape Minnow's accidental grasp. It went up over his eyes, as big as a plum, into his hair. He batted it off and heard it hit the ground and shamble off. The dog circled him, and he put one hand to the slightly swollen bite while pulling away the remaining web with the other.

He checked for the dog and saw its faint shape ahead in the brush. Minnow took a few steps forward, stumbling over his own feet. The bite throbbed, and he wondered what sort of spider it might have been. Black widows were tiny, not like that thing. He tried to walk again, then stopped and rubbed his eyes with his fists. When he opened them again, he saw the first haint.

A pale green orb lifted from near the ground, passing up through tree branches to a height well over his head. It drifted back and forth like a pendulum and then froze in midair. Its edges wisped and spiraled away from the dense core of light. It dipped and then floated away to his right, passing over the bluff, out of sight. The light had barely faded when another orb, this one pale yellow, floated from behind a wide trunk and then shrank to nothing as it slipped into the underbrush. It rose again and turned in place. Minnow's heart felt like a shard of ice pressed between his lungs. The thing flickered like a firefly, and when it went solid again a child's skull hung in the eerie light, patched with skin and tufts of hair on top, slack-jawed and gap-toothed. Then the light went out.

Minnow staggered backward and fell over the dog. The green orb rose over the dune's crest again and Minnow scrambled to his feet.

"Come on."

They fled into the woods. He looked over his shoulder and the green thing was gone. He wanted the openness of the river and the familiar bluff he'd scaled, but the green light might still be there. And besides, the river would be vast and gray and windy, and the bluff beaten by the wind.

He slapped past limbs and branches and trudged through the thick undergrowth of scrub palm and vines and weeds. Then a howl. A deep howl, starting low like a dog and then curling up into a whining scream. It sounded like it was right behind him—an arm's length—close enough that he could feel the hairs on his neck vibrate. He threw himself forward and whipped around to see its source.

Nothing. The dog cowered next to him against the ground with its heads between its paws. The branches shook from their passing, and the canopy shifted in hushed whispers with the wind, but all else was still.

"Come on."

He got to his feet and pressed into the woods, stepping high to fight through the underbrush. The dog sped up, and soon they were almost running through the woods. The crickets seemed muted, and the only sound came from their movement through the trees and bushes. The dog cut through twists of vines and sent low palm fronds flapping. Minnow moved silently, except for the whisper of branches brushing past his body. His breath came ragged, deep, as he tried to suck in needed air without making too much noise, without betraying his place in the trees. He looked over his shoulder and let his feet fall blindly. The woods took them in, and they lost sight of the sandy clearing or the bluff. His entire body braced for the howl again, but it never came.

He found no village. He pushed on through the woods with the dog, and the trees went on. The wind left them and the life of the river faded behind. The moon had set, or at least was blocked by the canopy, and the forest turned blacker. He tore through brambles and trudged through low wet muddy places that left his shoes packed with mud. The mud painted his legs black, and coated his clothes like thick tar. He crawled out of the worst of it on his hands and knees with the dog sitting and watching him. Once he was finally out, the dog slumped in a pile of leaves and closed its eyes.

"I don't think so," Minnow said, but he never stood up.

HE OPENED HIS EYES and a long millipede slid past his nose, flat and black and nighttime glossy. The forest was still, quiet, dark. The dog stood next to him, licking its paw. Minnow sat up, brushing off the dry edges of mud, and leaving the rest. When he flexed his shoes, mud flaked off like thick scabs. He thought of the blood his father coughed up the first night he went sick.

Minnow touched the spider bite and felt the swelling had passed. He stayed motionless and listened to a noise coming from the woods. The whole world was quiet, and now he could hear wind moving freely, maybe the sound of a bird in water. Something was up there. Maybe the edge of the island.

He stood and moved quietly through the trees, carefully picking past branches and vines. The dog followed him.

"You think they're still back there?" he asked.

The dog just kept following.

The world was dark. No gray dawn yet, and no moon to show the night's age. Cool air fell through the canopy. The breeze came back, and he rubbed his arms as he walked through the narrow trees. He put a hand out and gripped a cool, smooth trunk as he passed. The trees grew thinner, and the ground went soft again. Strands of green marsh grass sprouted at the edge of the woods. The land dropped away, and the trees ended at a shallow shelf. A marsh flat stretched out beyond: a wide field of silver dotted with shadowy hummock islands. The dark horizon was faint in the distance. It might have been night sky over the ocean, maybe more islands way out.

"Where would you put a village?"

The bluff on the right disappeared into the twilight at a backward curve, probably back around to where he had crossed the river. The dark shape of the forest curved out in front of them to the left, bordered by the quiet field.

"I'd build it on the banks."

The dog agreed, leaving the forest for the sandy shelf between the woods and the marsh. The low bluff was rough and dotted with saw palmettos, but it was a clearer path than through the woods. The dog led the way up the curve, following the island's edge. Minnow stepped carefully in his ruined shoes, sometimes up on the bluff's edge, sometimes down along the beach. In one place the bluff was too high and steep to climb without going back, and he had to pick through jagged clumps of oyster shells on the edge of the water. The pearly clumps showed sharp edges against the shadows, and the dog stopped to watch the shells squirt.

The bluff fell away again and then the land gave way to a wide expanse of water. It was like an inland sea, surrounded by the silver-green marsh, fed by some nearby creek or river. The inky water moved in the breeze, and the dark stirrings looked like rippled writing.

A duck took wing to his left, flying across his vision like a thrown dart. It began its upward turn and a shot rang out: a deep shotgun blast, and the world flashed and the duck plummeted into the water. A dog burst from a blind and ran down the lifeless thing, picking it up and returning to somewhere in the shadows.

The whole scene was a shadowy blur to Minnow, but he looked over his shoulder at the sky behind him. Maybe sunrise was soon. Maybe they were out early. He thought of the men back at the camp and wondered how far they could have come in the same time.

Minnow looked around and the dog was gone. Chasing the other one, maybe. Maybe spooked by the gunshot. Minnow stepped slow along the bank, following the land as it curved around the marsh inlet. They wouldn't see him, and that could be bad or good. They'd think he was a deer and blast him, or at least fire off a warning shot. His father always said not to shoot unless you knew what you were shooting at. Unless you were sure.

He froze. He listened for the dog, or for whoever was out there armed in the hidden blind. He took a step, and another, seeing the stark division of bluff and marsh. The grass grew tall, and the black water filled in all the space between the stalks. The world was still and quiet.

"Hello?" he whispered.

He looked to the trees over the path he'd come in on. Neither dog was there. He moved onto softer ground and gazed out over the marsh. A white egret took flight maybe half a mile away: a slender white shape against the dark.

"Hello?" he said louder.

"Who's that?" a quiet voice asked. A soft voice, trying to be quiet.

"My name's Minnow."

"Who are you?"

"I'm looking for someone."

"What?"

"I'm looking for someone."

"It's the middle of nowhere."

The voice came louder now, like someone had stood up to offer a hushed shout.

"Where are you?" the voice asked.

"I'm over on the edge. On the bluff."

"Keep walking."

He kept walking along the shore. He pressed through the darkness and came to a mud spit speckled with bricks. It might have once been a walkway to a dock or a shack on the marsh's edge. Now it was a slippery muddy arm stuck out into the water. He squinted to see the hunter but saw only shadow and marsh.

"Come on. I see you moving. Come down the mud."

He stepped across the bricks one by one and made his way down the broken causeway. When he looked back the dog was there again, sitting and watching him go.

"You stay there," Minnow whispered and turned ahead again. He saw a mud-splattered white bateau pulled up onto the slippery bank, sitting half out of the water. One man was visible to him, but the other was just a shape. The sight of the bone-white boat and the shadowy men made his guts turn.

"Come to us," the man said. The cut bottom of a tin can rested on the gunwale, and a stub of candle added a meager orange flicker to the shadows. The speaking man wore a floppy felt hat that bent down over his ears and curved up in the front. Dark overalls, a lighter colored undershirt. A shotgun at his shoulder, for hunting ducks, probably. The other man turned and almost seemed to creak when he did. He wore a dark leather jacket, and darkness hid the rest.

Minnow finished crossing the narrow band of mud and the shotgun man held out a hand to help him in. He stepped up into the boat and found it moored in the mud, unmoving even as he climbed in. The bow was stuck into the bank and the rest sat in a shallow inlet ringed by squirting oysters.

"I feel like I'm seeing a ghost out here this late," Shotgun said.

"You a ghost?" the other man asked. Minnow turned and faced him. He was in shadows, hidden from the candle. Minnow could see his pale face, though, and when his lips moved they revealed a gapped row of teeth.

"No sir. I came from Newfort. Looking for a village. I'm alive as you."

The old man laughed and Shotgun sat down, shouldering his weapon.

"Hope you didn't scare all the birds off," Shotgun said.

"I don't think so."

Minnow looked at the dog sitting at the back of the little boat. It was a mixed-breed with sharp ears and rusty brown fur. Much more elegant looking than his own companion.

"There ain't no village on this island," the man said.

"Someone told me to cross the river and look for it here."

"Who told you that?" Shotgun asked.

"And what river?" the older man laughed again at that.

"I'm not sure of that either."

"There used to be a village out here. Most folks left it and moved on to Saluskie, out west. A little settlement is farther out. A beach village. You think that's what they're talking about?" Shotgun asked.

"I'm not sure. How far is Saluskie?"

"Pretty far," the older man said.

"Maybe someone at the village will know something," Minnow said.

"Something about what?" the man asked.

"About what I'm looking for."

"And what is that?"

"Don't ask him too many questions or he'll run off. First company we ever had out here," Shotgun said.

"You're right," the man said.

"I'm looking for someone named Auntie Mae."

"Auntie Mae?" the man asked. He rubbed his head, covered in short white fuzz.

"Yessir."

"There's probably a hundred aunties and uncles out here. Most of them ain't nobody's aunt or uncle at all. How you going to find one? And at night too?" the man asked.

"I didn't mean to be going at night," Minnow said. "But I had to keep moving."

"Are you running from someone?" Shotgun asked.

"Something."

"And what's that?"

"You won't believe me."

"Well you can tell us anyway," the man said. He seemed to be looking at something out in the marsh. The dog too. Minnow turned to look and saw nothing.

"You believe in haints?"

"Haints?" Shotgun asked.

"Like ghosts. Or spirits."

Shotgun laughed this time and shook his head.

"Oh, I don't know," the old man said. "Plenty folks around here do."

"I had to run from them. In the woods on this same island."

"This island haunted?" Shotgun asked.

"I saw haints."

"All these islands is dangerous," the old man said, leaning his head down to look at the shadows in the bottom of the boat.

"Dangerous for ducks to be around here," Shotgun said.

"Quiet. They dangerous, and a lad like you shouldn't be out on them alone. No matter what you're looking for. Haints ain't it. Ghosts, demons. Things they call the plateye. Hidden like an animal and will follow you relentless. Real animals just as bad. Boar, rattlesnake."

"Plateye?" Minnow looked into the shadows of the bluff for the dog.

"You know when you see one. Fire in the eyes. Smoke all around. Dangerous things."

"Hush," Shotgun said.

"I'm just tryin' to warn him what's out there. These islands are old. You know that? Old since explorers been coming from across the water. Boats landed here. Frenchmen, Spaniards. Conquerers all. Killers. Murderers. Of entire people. Blood is out here. Brought with the slaves. Magic. Dark things."

Minnow shook his head. He looked over the men and imagined who they might know, or where they might tell him to go to be safe. He shook his head again.

"I'm fine. I just need help finding the village. Or Auntie Mae."

"And what's she going to tell you that's so important?" the old man asked. He picked up a tin mug and sipped something steaming.

"Something secret. Something I need."

"Well what is it?"

"Come on now," Shotgun said. "You gonna run him off faster than that dog can go."

Minnow looked at the dog.

"Fine then," the old man said.

"We should be asking if you're hungry."

Minnow nodded.

"Give him something," said Shotgun. "Sit down."

Minnow sat down on a bench next to the dog and the old man took out a tin lunch can like a miner might have. He opened it up and took out a biscuit and handed it to Minnow. Minnow broke it open. It was flaky and tender and salty on his tongue. He ate it all while the men watched and the dog watched closer.

"You drink coffee?" the old man asked.

"No sir," Minnow said, over his last swallow.

"Have water then. We got more of that anyway."

The old man poured the dregs out of an old leather cup and then filled it with water from a skin. He handed it to Minnow.

"Thank you. And for the biscuit."

Minnow drank the bitter water. His stomach loosened and he warmed. He felt good. He slumped back next to the dog and set his cup down.

"You can keep the cup," the man said.

"Thank you," Minnow whispered.

"Your father know where you are?" Shotgun asked.

"No sir."

"You see any ducks coming in?"

"No sir."

He leaned against the dog and the dog didn't move except to sigh.

"When was the last time you slept?" Shotgun asked.

"I slept in the woods."

"Braver than me," the man said.

The dog was wet, and his fur smelled mellow and musty. Minnow inhaled the pungent perfume and let his eyes sag to slits. The candle-flame danced, and the men cast their gaze over the gray marsh.

"If I were you, I'd follow the coast back around and cross the creek back to the Island," Shotgun said.

The words came to him almost floating on the thick marsh air, as if from all around at once.

"I can't, sir."

"He can't," the old man said. "So he should go up along the bluff. Cross Gowan's Creek where it gets skinny. Look for them people on that island. They might could help such a quest."

"Maybe so," Shotgun said.

"Yessir."

And he was asleep.

He dreamed of his father walking alone on a beach before a gray storm. The waves were gray, and the wind blew in over the ocean to make whitecaps like fingernail cuts in the water. His father wore a gray suit and a long gray beard hung from his face. Minnow followed his father along a high sandy dune that lost sand at its peak in swirling curls. Minnow called out to him, but the wind was too fierce. Each call made the wind louder, and he could not scream without waking up.

✺

MINNOW OPENED ONE EYE AND THEN the other, seeing only a dim gray world. The hull. The ribs of the boat. Marsh grass growing up around the edges, and a bit of silver water glowing in the early dawn. He put his hand up and felt the floppy hat that lay over his head, dipped low on his brow, blocking much of his view. He let his body move, and then stretched, feeling the dog next to him. Curly fur, though. Not the hunting dog. He sat up and the dog sat up with him, licking the side of his face and knocking the hat askew. He straightened it and looked to Shotgun and the old man, but they were not in the boat.

The shallow inlet had filled with water, and the sky was lightening with the first touch of dawn. Shadows still fell dark across the marsh grass, but the sun was rising on the distant horizon. The world was gray, damp, and misty, but the warm sun would be breaking the stillness soon.

Minnow sat up, rubbed his eyes, and scanned his surroundings again. He listened, maybe for the sound of their hunting dog, or the sound of the hunters themselves, trudging around in the marsh or shooting their guns.

Minnow touched the dog's fur to feel some piece of warm life. The boat was still. Water almost surrounded the dinghy, but it was run aground hard, stuck in the mud, and would never float again. The boat wasn't transportation, but just an old wreck they used for a blind.

The first rays of sun broke over the trees, and color returned to the world. Shotgun had left his hat. The bag was still in the boat, too. They couldn't have gone far. He stood in the boat and tried in vain to see over the tall grass.

A marsh hen cackled far away, and Minnow waited for another bird or another sound. When none came, he crossed the boat past the abandoned bag and stood there a moment.

He might wait for them, or call out. But now, under the sun, under the normal daylight, they might try to stop him or convince him to turn back. They would not understand his quest. Minnow folded the little leather cup and put it in his pocket.

"Thank you," he whispered. "Goodbye."

He stepped out onto the brick causeway, silent. The dog followed him and went ahead down the causeway to the bluff where the water lapped and licked. He followed the dog, and armies of fiddler crabs fled from his shadow. He reached the place where causeway met bluff and turned to look back at the boat, now framed red by the sun. Its dark silhouette sat on an endless field of sparkling marsh water. Minnow shielded his eyes and saw clouds in the sky with the sun, blood red and edged with amber. He dropped his hand, put his eyes to the ground, and moved on up the coast. He never heard the hunters fire a shot.

THE MORNING BRIGHTENED. He walked along the bluff until it fell into a sandy marsh-front beach. The dinghy disappeared in the grass and then behind a low hummock. He stopped on the beach and sat cross-legged in the sand. His legs were scraped from the underbrush, but his shoes were holding together, and he was mostly dry. The dog sat in front of him. Minnow took a piece of dried spartina and drew a circle in the shell-scattered sand. When he looked back up the dog was gnawing on something. Minnow opened his jaws and a slender gray bone dropped to the sand. It could have been from a long-dead raccoon, or a bird, or anything.

"What have you done?" Minnow asked.

The dog stooped down onto his front paws and then stretched out in the sand, chewing the tip of the bone like a toothpick.

"You know we can't keep going."

The dog looked up from the bone and then went back to chewing. The noise was like rocks grinding together.

Minnow drew a line through the circle in the sand. His stomach growled. The sun rose over the trees. The day began. His mother would wake up and know he was coming home. Maybe he got stuck out somewhere, or busy, or lost. She would wake up and know that he'd be back. He'd never missed a night before, but this could be his first. Everything would be fine.

"We can keep going a little bit. Maybe find the people across the creek. They said people were still up there."

A chill ran down his spine, and he looked over his shoulder again. A bird flew from a low hummock like something had scared it out of its rookery.

Minnow stood up and considered his sand drawing. He kicked it with his tattered shoes and squinted up at the sun. He shaded his eyes, and they walked together down the shell line. The dog left the bone at the place where they had stopped.

"Wish I had some of Mom's breakfast."

The dog's loping head seemed to be nodding.

"You never had it."

They walked on.

"It's good."

THEY WALKED NORTH ALONG a straight edge of beach and eventually reached the island's end. Not really an end, but a place where a wide creek cut the land in two. Fifty feet across, dark green, running with the tide into the sound, out toward the open ocean. It looked shallow, like it might empty out completely on a low tide.

"They said people might be over there still. Who didn't leave the village."

He gazed out over the creek. A high bluff led down from their place on the sandy beach. A steep drop a few feet, then shallow water leading out to the creek. Across the water was a sandy beach and a tall bluff with palmetto trees leaning over from behind. The sky overhead was clear blue, and the ocean off to the right was cobalt to match.

"I don't feel much like swimming."

The dog moved ahead and pawed at the sharp bluff edge.

"No boat either."

The dog jumped down the bluff and scrambled along the last little ledge between water and land.

"Careful."

Minnow scanned the creek and then the wider marsh flat to his left. More land out there, more islands over the same flat that the hunters hunted on. To his right the curve of the island disappeared, leaving only creek, sound, and ocean. Nothing but deeper water that way, with treacherous currents and undertows.

"We could wait for low tide. Get across then."

The dog looked up at him. Minnow thought of his father in bed. His mother hoping he would return. Knowing he would.

"Can't wait for that."

The dog yawned.

"Guess we're swimming."

He checked his belongings and slid down the sandy bluff to the creek's edge. It was shallow and muddy for a time, then dark at a drop off. The water moved swiftly, out toward the ocean.

"Shoes or no shoes?"

The dog jumped in with legs extended. Minnow dove in after him, splashing into the shallow water and then gliding out into the dark creek. He breast-stroked, letting the current draw him out as he fought for forward progress. The dog was just a shaggy head on the surface, cutting a wake in the water toward the beach. The current pulled them both and the dog adjusted its angle.

Minnow kicked and one of his shoes went loose at the ankle. Water moved in and out of the split seams and the suction took the first shoe off. It unbalanced his kicks and he slipped the other shoe off and let it sink, let it float to the dark depth of the creek. He imagined what might be in a creek so close to the open ocean. A leviathan. A giant ray. Some many-armed creature from the fathoms. Sharks. Sharks in the sound, looking for creatures drawn out by the current of the creek. Sharks feeding in swarms where the water got deep and cold.

His bare feet felt exposed in the water and he kicked harder, making distance up against the dog. He reached the edge on the other side with ragged breaths. He pushed harder and stroked into the shallows.

Minnow dragged himself up the beach, shoeless, soaking, hair plastered to his face. The dog followed right behind, treading lightly up the sand. Minnow flipped over and let the water sling off his body. He lay prostrate on the warm sand with his limbs outstretched. The dog sat down next to him and started licking its drooping curls.

⚹

The sun shined down and warmed him. The breeze blew, shaking palm fronds above and behind. The forest whispered. A fine mist of sand blew along the top of the beach and stung his skin, and then the wind left and the beach was still and hot. A gull clucked and croaked from a hidden roost.

He lifted his head up and looked back across the creek at the wild island he'd just left. It seemed peaceful, abandoned, quiet. Behind him the dunes rose twice as tall as he was, white sand crested by spindly sea oats waving in the occasional breeze. The palmetto trees suggested woods on the other side, but a jungle was more likely. It would be hard to pass through without a trail, but it would also be shady and cool.

He lifted himself to escape the heat of the sand and limped to the edge of the dunes. The dog stayed in the sun, licking. The beach wound off between water and bluff for as far as he could see in either direction. Ocean stretched out one way, and the other way was everything else: the islands and the marshes and somewhere way out was Newfort and everything he'd left. The bluff, Bay Street, the road to his house. The grass out front hot and dry in the sun. The house cool and dark. Candlelit. A day had passed since he'd left. He glanced back and thought of Sorry George watching him. Three things coming his way.

He wondered whether he had met one yet.

He walked up the beach with the ocean in front of him, out in the distance. The dog went ahead, stopping to poke its snout into ghost-crab holes or nudge drifts of crackling spartina over the sand with one paw. Minnow scanned the tree line over the bluff for gaps or places where he might enter the woods, but the palm tree crowns grew close and tight. A jungle. An island jungle. No one would build a village in that.

"You think anyone would build in there? Stay in there?"

He walked on with the dog right in line ahead of him. It stopped to sniff some game tracks set in the sand.

"No. You'd build on the beach. Next to the water. Probably next to a creek."

He kicked the bleached half of a clam.

"Probably all gone."

They followed the beach. The ocean lay off to the right, with the undulating dunes guarding the left. A wind came from over the open water and swayed the dark forest beyond.

"What time is it?"

The dog glanced back at him and then continued on.

"You hungry? What have you been eating?"

The dog did not respond.

"It's probably close to lunch. No shrimp plates out here."

The thought brought him to walk in the water's edge. The foaming edge cooled his feet, but any thought of seeing something to eat was silly, he knew. Minnows darted where the water rose deeper with the gentle waves, but nothing was there to eat.

The dog barked. Minnow snapped his head up. The dog's neck was angled sharply as it looked over a low dune into the woods. Minnow scanned the trees, but everything moved and shook in the breeze, and nothing seemed out of place to him. Just the green island jungle.

The enormity of it rose in his mind. The towering trees, the dunes. The ocean behind him. The waves building against the shore. Waves. Not the river, not a creek.

"How far do you think we've come out?"

The dog looked away from the trees, back at him. They continued down the sand.

The sun hit a high spot over their heads, and they moved up to the bluff and walked in a narrow line of shade offered by the palmetto crowns on the other side. The skin on the back of Minnow's neck felt tight and hot from burn. He would not be home for a long time. The sunburn couldn't be allowed to get worse, or he would be in bad trouble. They couldn't stay on the beach all day.

He rubbed the burned spot on his neck and squinted.

"I'm pretty hot. And hungry."

He scanned the bluff, the tree line, like food might be growing right there. Only birds. A few birds, and an empty world. A gull called overhead and he glanced up to see it. Then he stumbled, tripping on the sharp stump of an ancient beach tree. He fell forward and caught himself in the sand with the heels of his palms. The dog stopped and turned fast and trotted back.

"I'm all right."

He stood up and brushed off his knees and his hands. He adjusted his shirt hem and pressed his hands on his chest, then his stomach. He felt his arms and his muscles and squeezed his shoulders with his hands.

They continued on and they both dried out. His clothes stayed stiff, wrinkled, salt-stained. The sun felt hotter for their dryness, even in the shade, but soon the sun would be falling. Soon it would be retreating and giving them mercy.

The dog left the shade to sniff a line of tracks at the water's edge. The bluff diminished as they continued, turning from a high cliff of sand to a low ridge, and then to nothing more than a gentle rise on the beach. The woods were right there, palmetto and pine, twisted with vines and moss. Little shadowy trails showed along the edge, made by game or man or perhaps something else. They walked faster, now out of the sun, moving in the full shade of the jungle.

The dog stopped up ahead on the beach, dipped its nose in the water, and then went up to the trees. It barked, circled once, and retreated down to the water's edge. Minnow broke away from the woods as he approached the place the dog had stopped. He watched the jungle's dim interior, watched its rustling edge.

"What are you looking at?" he asked the dog, without taking his eyes off of the trees. He followed the dog down the water line, picking up a weaving set of tracks. The water crept up and washed over some of the outliers. He still saw them, though: sharp hooves, set deep in the soft sand, edges still sharp. He was no expert tracker, but they were too close together for a deer.

The brush exploded and a boar was right on them: a bloated brown hog with a line of spiked fur down its back and two brown tusks jutting from its maw. One of them was splintered and jagged, and the other one was curved in a wicked hook.

The dog doubled back and ran between Minnow and the beast, charging it for a second before veering off in the direction they'd come. Minnow ran ahead, down the line of tracks, splashing through the water. The boar turned for the dog, as Minnow had hoped, but didn't waste long pursuing that game. It spun and pawed the sand once and then came full speed after Minnow. Minnow glanced back just long enough to see its beady black eyes rolling in its giant wrinkled head.

Minnow ran out of the water and pounded his feet across the packed sand higher up. He had to use the space the dog had bought him, and it was all he was going to get. The mutt had turned and was in pursuit, but its tiny legs would not carry it fast enough to overtake them, or even keep up.

Minnow eyed the tree line. He wasn't going to outrun the hog. He heard the sand flying and heard the hog grunt and moan. It squealed a high scream as it bore down on him. He'd heard stories of boar on the islands and how they would put their tusks between your legs and shake their head. How nothing of you below the waist would be left.

He had no choice. He cut a diagonal path toward the trees and stole a glance over his shoulder at the rampaging animal tearing a rut in the sand. The dog was back there too, following in the rut, but falling behind.

He turned back and he was in the trees. He slipped between a narrow gap in the line of palmetto trunks and crashed into the jungle, but the inner wall of branches and moss bounced him back toward the beach. The pig squealed, and he knew he'd lost his lead. He dove low and scrambled under everything, crawling like a lizard beneath brush and vine and branch, expecting to feel the boar on him at any moment.

Minnow tunneled through the foliage and emerged into a clear slot in the dense jungle. He ran for a small palmetto, only twice his height. The boar squealed, right behind him, and Minnow sprang up into the tree where he hid in the bottom of the dense crown, ten feet up. He looked down and the boar was right there, a swollen sack of shaking brown flesh clawing at the palmetto, squealing and grunting and then digging and pawing at the trunk. It rammed against the tree and the tree shook and swayed.

Minnow looked up at the canopy and the blue sky breaking through. In that moment he wondered what his mother would think of him, up in the tree.

The pig actually scrambled up into the low stalks on the side of the tree, and Minnow's heart froze. He could smell its breath and feel the warmth coming off its skin. The hog fell clumsily back down to the earth and started snorting at the base of the trunk. It rammed the trunk a few more times, slamming the top of its head against the wood. It turned its snout up and showed a face streaked with blood and drool.

The dog came barking, crashing through the brush, not slowing at all as it tore past the boar and snapped the air next to its head. The boar took off after the dog and Minnow listened and watched as they ripped a path through the thick undergrowth.

He settled in the fronds and checked himself for wounds. Scratches from the quick ascent, one of them pretty deep.

Nothing else. He listened to the animals chasing each other through the forest. They had gone far, but now were circling back toward him and the tree. He briefly checked the trunk as if checking a ship at sea before a storm.

He was still listening to the sound of their chase when the second boar came up from the beach, snorting and grunting and then stopping to smell around the trunk. It lifted its head up, looking for its prey, and then cocked its head to catch the faint barking that reached the otherwise quiet piece of woods. It was a male too, bigger than the first by half. Drool dripped from its hanging lip flaps and made its splintered tusks glisten. Minnow didn't know if it saw him. He stayed still. Then the boar squealed and turned a circle and looked up at him. It shook its head as if to show what its tusks could do.

Then it rammed. Like the other one, but harder. Heavier. The tree shook as in an earthquake.

"Go away!"

It rammed again and a stalk from the side of the tree broke loose. The trunk shifted and Minnow could see where the shallow root ball had lifted an edge of soil at the base.

"Get!"

The second boar rammed once more, then circled the trunk, then started ramming and butting from another angle. This time a fury of butting: hitting and hitting and slamming the palmetto until its head bled and coated the lower trunk with black blood.

"Dog! Dog!"

The boar kept butting at the tree, then tearing at the ground with its bloody hooves and tusks. It went around to its first place of attack and backed up to ram the tree again. This time the frail palmetto leaned under Minnow's weight. The hog backed up to see its progress, and Minnow saw that the root ball had lifted more, a shelf of earth exposing a dark crack beneath. Minnow looked over his shoulder and did not see the dog. The tree was going to fall. He would have to run, or he would have to stand and fight.

"Dog!"

He searched around the tree for anything, for a good stick, for the stem of a frond still intact. He pulled one and flexed it until it broke. The hog rammed again and Minnow was not ready. He scrambled to hold on, then looked down. The thing was still there, puffing and breathing and preparing for another hit.

Then he felt the arrowhead, pressed into his thigh. He reached in and took it out: gray flint, brittle, but still sharp. One of the biggest he'd ever seen, almost as long as his palm, flaring out from a stabbing point into a wide V shape with a stub on the bottom that would fit an arrow shaft. He held it like a dagger. The hog rammed the tree again and seemed to know Minnow was watching, because it turned its broad head up and squealed a final taunt. It opened its slobbering mouth to show rows of stubby teeth and then shook again, flinging blood and drool and waving long tusks at Minnow.

"Come on! Come on!"

It rammed again, and again. It pawed the earth, and Minnow heard the tree groaning at the roots. The fronds rustled and the boar reared back for another ram, and Minnow jumped out as it did. The last blow sent the tree backward, out from under him, but he had already jumped and now plummeted down with the arrowhead gripped in both hands like a knife. He crashed through a spiky knot of branches, twisted in the air, and landed on the beast. Minnow plunged the arrowhead down into its neck, pushing it deep until he felt a bone.

The thing squealed and bucked him off with one wild whip of its body. It pawed the ground once, twice, shook its tusks, and charged. It made five great gallops and then its eyes went gray and its head thumped down into the ground. Its body collapsed. The boar took one last great wheezing breath and died. The arrowhead stayed stuck in its neck, a notch of flint protruding from the quivering flesh.

Minnow screamed and curled up into a ball in the leaves, grabbing at his face and the deep scratches cut into his right check. And something else. Something stuck in his face. He tried to move, tried to look at the hog to make sure it was still dead, but his head spun and his stomach pushed hot stuff up into his mouth.

"Dog!" he screamed.

He put his hand to his face and pulled it away with blood on his fingers. He wanted to close his eyes and stop. He wanted to stop and never move again. He was bleeding bad from his face, from somewhere on his face, and he could still feel the heat of the hog on his skin. His heart raced, and his head spun. He didn't want to move again, but then he thought of his father. He took a deep breath and stayed still on the ground, watching the hog's body. He listened for the dog. His heart thumped loud inside his ears. But he had to move. He knew it.

Minnow rolled onto his back, then his side, and white stars bounced across his vision. He shook his head to clear the flashing lights away. He tried to rise up, but the stars swirled in his vision again like the sparkling remnants of a firework. He dropped down, slamming his back into the ground. The wind left him and he stared at the gaps of blue through the treetops. He cursed the pig, which he could now smell like feces and trash and blood. He breathed and listened to the sound of his breathing.

A distant bark.

"Dog," he said.

The stars left his eyes, but something remained in the corner of his vision. He put his hand up and brushed the twig that jutted from the fleshy inside corner of his right eye. A lightning-bolt of pain shot into his head where the stick was rooted in his face. Between the tree and the hog's back and the ground, he'd found the bare branches of a water oak. Part of a branch was in his face, now.

He tried to see the thing in the corner of his eye, but it was only a dark shape just out of sight. He moved his fingers to it, tried to hold them still. He pinched it and pulled it out, a splinter as long as his pinky, half its length coated in blood. Blood trickled from the pinhole it left empty. He put three fingers against the tiny hole to stem the bleeding, and the world spun around him.

The sun moved over his head. He lay motionless next to the hog in the bloody brush. He couldn't tell how long. He closed his eyes, and the last thing he thought was that Varn might be mad if he didn't bring the arrowhead back.

SOMEONE SQUEEZED HIS SHOULDERS, then dragged him. His legs scraped across pine needles and roots. His head lolled, and his vision faded. Something dug beneath him, pushed, then lifted him up. His head fell back and his hair left his eyes. He saw the dark man's silhouette, darker for the sun behind him.

"What he got on his face?"

"Looks like the pig got him."

"I mean on his face."

"Cuts."

"He got something else by his eye."

"I see it now. Don't look good."

He groaned and a cool palm cupped his cheek. Someone hushed him, he closed his eyes, and it was night all around.

The night brought mist and humid air. It roiled in from the sea and blew over the islands like a long, warm breath. Minnow lay on a cot that cradled his body. He lay in a fever, tracing the hammock of reeds, feeling the way the edges interlocked. Someone spooned hot soup into his mouth. Chicken. Salt. He drank it deep and breathed the thick air.

After he ate he felt sleepy. A breeze blew in from far away, cool over his body and cool over the entire world. The wind smelled of salt and sea, bringing the tale of faraway waves. Someone cleaned his face with a cool cloth. Gentle pressure squeezed water out to run over his cuts. Someone dried him.

Careful fingers checked pink wounds and applied cotton cloth and a smelly salve. He shivered.

"Run that dog off. Bothering my chickens."

He woke on his side, facing the sunrise over a long yellow beach. A broad river lapped at the beach, sparse marsh grass growing where water met sand. More islands, just dark tree lines, far across the river.

Huts stood along the tree line. A rooster crowed, and he saw a chicken scratching in the sand nearby. A few children ran along the water's edge, splashing. A man with a net yelled something at them and they went off. The man picked the net up and held one edge in his teeth and spun it through the air into a dark hollow of water. It splashed, and he brought it back with the line tied to his wrist.

Minnow's head throbbed. He sat up and rubbed his left eye, then carefully trailed his fingers along his right cheek. He felt three deep cuts, each as long as his longest finger. Three deep cuts, and the dull throb in the corner of his right eye. A black blur swam around the bottom of his vision. He put his hand to the eye and pressed one finger against the place where the twig had stabbed him. He felt a small, hard scab. The flesh beneath the scab was tender. He stood up and put weight on his sore legs. His head spun. He clenched his teeth and tried a few steps.

"Walkin' off on us already?" a woman asked.

He froze. He thought of everyone he'd met so far. He thought of the trouble and the danger. But these people had taken him to their village. They'd taken him away from the rotting, dead pig and fed him and fixed up his face.

He turned to face a negro woman not much older than his mother. Dark skin, narrow body, thin, like a willow tree. A white cloth wrapped the top of her head and covered her hair. Her white dress hung loose, flowing around her like an elegant gown.

"No ma'am. Just testing out my legs."

"How's your eye?"

"It feels all right."

"Babo and Jim found you out there in the woods. They was hunting but found you instead. You get in a mess with them pigs?"

Minnow nodded.

"They everywhere out there."

"Have you seen my dog?"

"That runt?" the woman asked, nodding her head up the beach. Minnow turned and saw a ragged dog shape chasing through a group of children. Minnow nodded.

"He's bothering the chickens. He better not eat one," she said.

"He may, if he doesn't get food."

"We fed 'im scraps."

"Thank you."

"You lucky to be walking still. Walking with the living at all. What are you doing on this island?"

"I came from town. I'm trying to help my father. He's sick."

Minnow closed his right eye and winced. A tear formed in the hurt corner. He looked over his shoulder at the river to hide it.

"Sit down. If it hurts."

He shook his head.

"I can't stay. I can't stay long."

"He that sick?"

"Yes ma'am. He's dying."

"And how is this island going to help him?"

"I'm looking for Auntie Mae. She knows something that I need to know. Someone in Frogmore told me she might be living out here. In a village. On this island."

"You got the village. But there ain't no Auntie Mae."

"What?"

"You hard of hearing?"

"No ma'am. But I'm sure she's out here."

"Oh she out here. But buried. She been dead for goin' on a year now."

Minnow staggered but caught himself.

"You all right?"

"Yes ma'am."

"What's your name? Tell me your name."

"Minnow."

"Like the fish?"

Minnow nodded.

"Like the little one," she said.

Minnow looked over and saw the dog sitting on its haunches, just a shadow framed by the rising sun. A child sat with it in the sand, rubbing its head.

"My name is Gretel. Auntie Mae was my great-grand-mother, or great-great. What you need to know that Auntie Mae knew? Maybe someone still knows it."

Minnow sucked his bottom lip between his teeth. He looked back at the dog.

"Come on, now," she said. "You think we can't help? Can't trust us. You came all this way to our island. Lookin'."

Minnow nodded.

"I'm looking for Sorry George's grave."

Gretel put her hand on her chest and stepped away.

"Why you looking for that?"

"I need dirt from his grave. To pay a debt. To get medicine for my father. In Port Royal."

"Port Royal?"

Minnow nodded.

"You been on quite a trip. You know where you are?"

Minnow shook his head.

"You way out. But you come to the right place. I can't help you. But someone here might know."

Minnow opened his mouth to thank her, but just took in a deep breath and shook his head. He couldn't believe hope was still possible. Someone might know. All this way, and Auntie Mae dead. But still hope, alive.

"When? When can we find them? I've been gone so long from town."

"You need to take it slow, though," Gretel said. "We'll find them soon. Gonna be a big feast tonight. Big time. Everyone will be there. We'll find out then."

"I don't know if I have that much time," Minnow said. He looked at the still-rising sun. It couldn't be much later than ten, eleven in the morning. It was a long time till dinner.

"Maybe you meant to slow down. That's why we here. To slow you down. Maybe get you ready for what comes ahead. If you really planning on going to the grave, you gonna need to think it over."

She held his hand and they walked up the beach. Her hand felt like his mother's, and he squeezed it. She released, and slowed down. He walked slow too, limping from a pulled muscle in his leg. He walked careful, still a little dizzy. She stopped, and he didn't notice at first. He kept going, looking at the shell line, and when he glanced back she was gone. He walked on, then stopped at the dog and a boy.

"Hello," the negro boy said. He was dressed much like Minnow: barefoot, short pants, thin white shirt now colored gray. Skin dark, like chocolate. Hair a wild round circle, uncombed. A year or two younger than Minnow.

"Hello."

"Who are you?"

"I'm Minnow."

"I'm Cory."

"That's my dog."

The child looked at the dog like it was hiding a secret.

"This dog?"

"Yes. It's been with me since town."

"It's scrawny."

"I know."

Minnow patted the dog and gazed up the beach. The man with the net was there. A few pine plank structures straddled the water line on foundations of tall pine poles. Palmetto fronds shaded roofs of rough wooden shingles. The empty beach stretched beyond.

"Where's the village?"

"Up in the woods."

"Do a lot of people live here?"

The boy squinted his eyes and looked Minnow up and down.

"My whole family. A lot of families. We're all family. What you doing here? Come to get your dog?"

Minnow shook his head.

"I'm here for the meal. Gretel invited me to a feast."

The boy closed his eyes and nodded and made a humming sound.

"It's gonna be a feast, too," he said. "I'll look for you if you want. You can sit with me."

"I'll look for you, too."

"Where you going now?" Cory asked.

"To the village, I guess. I'd like to see it."

The boy nodded.

"I'll come back," he told the dog, and it stayed put, lying on all fours, panting, staring at the river and the marsh flats beyond.

Minnow waved a hand at the mutt and left.

He walked up the beach, over a low dune, past the three structures on the water line. They were like high dock heads, built over the ground with rickety-looking stairs leading up to each platform. Railings guarded the sides, sanded planks made the floors, and each open porch had its own rough-shingled roof embellished with palm fronds. Benches and tables and stools sat in the shade under the roofs, but the verandas were empty of people at the moment. All three were built in such a way—and made high enough—to stand over the river's edge during the high tide.

He walked down a well-trod path to the village proper: a dozen or so huts built up in a sandy clearing in the pine forest. Trails led around to each hut, and a central gathering place was cleared in the middle. At the middle of that, a fire pit. Smaller fires burned all around, some with food or cauldrons heating on the flames. A shaggy dog scampered by. A couple of children played in a dirt circle at the edge of the huts. One woman, light-skinned, sat in a rocking chair, knitting. Birds sang everywhere in the jungle around them, lighting the air with their varied voices. Dark ruts led off into the dense jungle in every direction.

He passed a clutch of chickens clawing at the sandy ground, pecking through long orange pine needles. A man passed him and considered Minnow an extra moment, but then just smiled and kept on his way. Minnow looked back to see him, but the man did not stop.

He arrived at the center of the village and the clearing at the middle. He sat on a pine bench and checked his belongings: flask, still full, tucked in the leather pouch. The leather cup from the hunters. His last money: one dented quarter and a dirty dime. Shoes gone. Feet all right, but leg aching. His eye ached too, but he pushed the pain away with thoughts of his father. Minnow was salty, sandy. His dirty hair hung in tangles and clumps that would probably have to be cut out. His nose felt pink and burned to the touch, and his neck too. He pocketed his things and smoothed his hair the best he could. He was all right. He would go on.

A few people moved around the huts, but not many. Most folks were probably out doing whatever they did in a day. This was just another normal sunrise for them, a normal day. For him it was not. For him, the clock was ticking, and one more day would be gone before he would be back home. Back to Frogmore. To the Ferry.

He left the glowing pit of coals and walked the village perimeter, maybe hoping someone would stop him or talk to him or offer food. No one did. He passed the children playing in the dirt, and they glanced up and then ignored him. The other handful of souls he passed did the same, exchanging maybe a mild smile or a quiet hello. He did not see Gretel.

Each hut was different. They were all well-built, constructed on low pilings that left a few feet of air between the ground and the floor. Most of them had porches, with pine-pole walls and palm fronds over wooden shingles. A big building made of logs looked like a gathering hall, and a small log chapel had a golden cross mounted atop of the roof. The village existed far out on the islands, but Minnow could see it was alive and thriving. He came back around to the beach path and went up to the sand again. The dog and Cory were still there.

"See anyone?" the boy asked.

Minnow shook his head.

"Wait until tonight. You come all this way for a feast? You must be good friends with Gretel to come here from town."

"I'm here for more than that. Trying to help my father. He's sick."

"Sick?"

"Yes."

"And you came out here to help him?"

"Yes."

"They didn't have the medicine in town?"

"Not exactly."

"Must be something special. How long you been out here?"

"A few days."

"Alone?"

"With the dog, part of the way."

"He much help?"

"He has been."

Cory looked Minnow up and down, and looked at the cuts on his face.

"You all right? Your face don't look good."

"It's hurt, but it's not too bad." Minnow tried not to think about the itching he felt in the corner of his right eye.

"Let's walk," Cory said. "Let me take you up the beach."

Cory got up, but the dog stayed put. Minnow watched the boy walk up the beach and then turned to the dog.

"You coming?" he asked.

The dog followed.

They walked, and the sky over the island turned copper, then red. Purple feathers brushed away the red, and wisps of gray followed. A pale moon rose. The sky went black, and the stars hung overhead like an endless net of crystals. The water licked the shore in slow hushes, and the air settled warm and still all around. Drums sounded in the distance, far away, across many islands. They beat a low rhythm with the waves, but no one at the village seemed to notice. A breeze stirred the air, just enough to calm Minnow and cool his skin. He walked with Cory down the beach to the porches on the water line.

The dog played at the foot of one of the porches with two village pups, and a few children wrestled nearby. A man arrived from the village trail, tall and lean and just a shadow in the night. He began lighting candles around the porches, and the children stopped to watch. He lit resin torches mounted on the railings and then sparked a half-dozen lamps scattered around on broad tables. The light built into a shimmering golden halo that illuminated the yellow sand and the jungle's green edge. Lamplight caught the crowns of the high palmetto trees that rustled in the breeze.

The man lit torches on the beach. They cast a glow over the sand and the dark water. He lit more torches, leading up and along the trail. The gathering place on the beach glittered with light, but even then the man was not done. He scaled the single live oak that sent its spidery arms around the three porches and scooted from branch to branch, lighting fat candles in clay cups. The candles put off smoky yellow flickers, and the leaves and the moss around the porches were lit as if in early morning. Someone watching from a distant island might have thought the jungle was aflame, blazing with torches and candles and lamps.

More villagers arrived. They swept and prepared tables and pulled benches and stools into place. Even more people gathered on the beach below, grouping together at an open space next to one of the porches. They lit a bonfire and made smaller fires, over which they built spits. They toiled in the light of the torches, readying their kitchen.

Cory ran off, but Minnow stayed near the tree line, watching the crowd move and talk and wait. Then the catch arrived: a harvest from the sea brought in baskets and pots and nets slung over shoulders. The whole place smelled salty and fresh as the haul was spread on work tables and dumped into cooking pots on the beach. Men and women began the work of cleaning and preparing the catch, stopping to exclaim over a particularly rusty crab or an especially fat fish. Pots of water boiled over fires, pans warmed on coals, and men knelt to fan the heat.

People streamed out of the forest trail from the village. They came from up the beach, and from down the beach: slim black shadows emerging from gray into gold. The men were mostly shirtless, wearing knickers or loose, billowing pants. The women came in colorful dresses that flowed around them like flower petals and stopped at the knee. Everyone came barefoot, meeting and embracing and exclaiming with laughter and discussion as if they had not seen each other for years. The beach filled with people, but the high porches remained empty.

Minnow found the dog, lying exhausted on the sand, and then Gretel found them both.

"Are you ready?"

"Yes ma'am. Hungry."

"You will help begin the meal," she said.

"How do you mean?"

"You are our guest tonight."

Minnow observed the crowd. It had become still, except at the kitchens. People turned to look at him, and a hush fell over the beach. He drew close to Gretel and put his hand on the dog's head. He scanned the crowd and saw strange faces, staring, quiet. He felt that everyone on the beach was looking at the cuts on his face.

"You will help begin the meal."

Minnow nodded, and swayed. He put a hand to his temple.

"Minnow!"

He saw Cory push through the crowd to join them.

"You found me," Minnow whispered as Cory took his hand. Cory rubbed the dog's head and smiled up at Minnow.

"You're not that hard to find," Cory said, and lifted their clasped hands.

"I guess not."

"Come on."

Cory took him by the hand and led him up the stairs of the nearest porch. They took places on a bench before a long plank table. The other two porches filled with people—talking, murmuring, gathering around the tables, perching on stools, sitting up on the railings. Someone boosted a little girl onto a long limb of the live oak, where she sat before a glowing candle. Only Gretel joined them on the first porch. She stayed off to one side, leaning against a railing, watching them at the middle table. Then came the food.

A train of people carried the feast up from the beach kitchens. They brought overflowing baskets of boiled shrimp and boiled crab, seasoned spicy red. Women laid out platters piled high with cobs of sweet white corn, roasted and sprinkled with salt. Men passed along sweetgrass bowls filled with shrimp fried in a golden batter, served with a rainbow array of sauces. Plates of fish were made in all ways: seared as thin filets, kept whole and crusted with salt and spices, fried in golden batter, some made into a thick, delicious stew. Cornbread came stacked in pyramids, cooked dark with dark crispy edges. Each board of bread came with a basket of fritters, fried brown and still steaming. A line of children followed the adults, carrying bowls of rice mixed with shrimp and spices. A giant man brought in two barrels, one on each shoulder, and women set bottles and jugs out on the tables. And more baskets. Baskets and baskets of the boiled bounty.

The procession ended. A beautiful chocolate-skinned woman stood at the head of their table with a basket in her arms. The porch was full now—packed with children and women and men and one dog—but the crowds across all three porches had gone quiet, waiting. The woman smiled at them, lifting one hand while holding the basket against her hip. Someone called out from another porch, and she leaned forward and spilled the contents of the basket across the table. The shrimp and crab flowed out in a glistening, steaming tide. Spicy steam roiled into the air and out over the beach. The bounty was spread before them: orange shrimp in shells, crab claws sharp and red, tender white bodies split, legs curled by the heat. Each salty piece was fat with flaky, succulent flesh.

The beach was silent. Cory nudged Minnow.

"What are you waiting for?"

Minnow put out a hand and took one shrimp in his fingers: a fat shrimp as long as his palm, cooked in the shell with its tiny black eyes and long red whiskers still on. Flecks of spice colored the plates of its armor. He pinched the legs and peeled the shell off. The body was pink, tinged orange, curled inward. The biggest shrimp he'd ever seen. It took three bites to eat, even for him, and it was sweet and salty with a smoky red spice that lingered on his tongue.

He woke from the first taste and everyone at the table had joined in. People had taken places all around: eating at other tables, eating on the railings, or eating standing up. Gretel sat at their table with a dozen more, all digging into the steaming shrimp and crab. A man uncorked a slender bottle and poured icy water into a wooden mug in front of Minnow. Minnow tipped the mug and drained it, cooling his throat, his body, and his burning cheek. He put the mug down and it was filled again. Someone tossed a cracked claw over to Minnow. The exposed white meat glistened with melted butter. He picked it up, studied it, and ate the meat off the claw. Cory had already amassed quite a pile of cracked crabs and empty shells. He reached into a basket and handed Minnow one of the golden-brown fritters.

"Hushpuppy," Cory mumbled, through his full mouth. Minnow took it and ate the sweet fried dough. It was like a corn fritter, fried with a little spice, and crafted to prepare his palate for more shrimp.

The feast went on across the three porches, and people ate, and drank, and toasted. They laughed and talked as they picked at the food spread before them. They shared bites and traded claws and suggested particular morsels of fish. They passed bottles around, sometimes throwing them between porches, sometimes hanging them upside down from tree branches when they were spent.

Another platter of fish arrived at their table, and Minnow took a filet of flounder, grilled, flavored with lemon slices and butter. He ate it with eyes closed, succulent like the sea itself, and thanked the warm air and the river before them for the wonderful meal. He opened his eyes and looked at the people who had labored, cooked, and then eaten with him. He opened his mouth to speak, but the place was loud, raucous, and a song began at the center porch. It might have started up in the trees, but by the time Minnow stood to listen the song had taken the entire middle porch and was spreading. All three porches joined at once in the song: low and quiet, joyful. No song Minnow had ever heard. It spread out of the jungle's edge, high over the sandy beach, and far across the dark water.

People returned to their food and the noise began again. Beer and wine had been flowing for some time, and men and women alike were louder and showed bigger smiles. Jokes rang loud and people laughed. A round of riddles began, with voices jumping from porch to porch. A woman next to Minnow leaned in and said: "The more it eats, the larger it gits. The larger it gits, the more it eats. Wha' dat?"

Minnow thought, then shook his head.

"A fire!" Cory yelled.

The woman laughed and returned to her plate.

A sweet voice sang out another riddle, like a poem: "Chick willa high, chick willa low. No man can clim' chick willa." No one answered for a moment. Laughter, commotion, then someone called out: "Smoke!"

"Like from a chimney," Cory said.

"Like from a chimney," Minnow repeated, watching a plate of squid go by, sliced into circles, simmered in rich grease and dusted with pepper.

The jokes and the laughing and the riddles went on. Two men battled back and forth with questions, eventually rising up on their benches, chests gleaming with sweat, faces stern, riddles flying between them, the crowd hushed. They finished with a riddle that no one on any of the three porches could answer, and that man won. He gave an exaggerated bow and embraced his competitor. The porches applauded, and everyone returned to eating.

The moon set, and the feasting slowed. The candles burned low, and the lamps faded down as people finished eating and began pushing away from the tables. Men lit pipes and cigarettes and the women took children into their laps. The stories began. Minnow didn't know if they were telling them on the other porches, but on his porch a gray old man pulled up a stool and lit a corncob pipe. He puffed rings of gray smoke and began a story about a haint that lived on a nearby island. Minnow listened, but someone came behind him.

"Minnow," Gretel said.

He turned from the tale and looked at her.

"I have someone you will want to talk to."

Minnow glanced back at the storyteller, wanting to hear how it ended, but then remembered his true quest. He wiped his hands on his pants, barely cleaning them at all, and followed Gretel back into the crowd. The whole porch was quiet, with everyone listening to the tale.

Gretel brought him to the back railing where a few people smoked, and a few couples kissed and rubbed each other. A short wide man stood in the shadows with his arms crossed. He wore a dented floppy hat that drooped to one side, but when Minnow got close enough his face looked grim and taut and did not match the hat.

"This is Petruchio."

"Hello," Minnow said.

"This is the boy I told you about," Gretel said.

"Minnow. Like a little fish."

"Yessir."

"What's a little fish got any business looking for Sorry George?"

Something squeezed his heart inside his chest. The name had power, and the man had said it. No mystery, no tricks. Just the name. If he was willing to talk, so was Minnow.

"Doctor Crow sent me to get dust from his grave. In exchange for medicine."

Petruchio laughed and put a hand on his belly. Then his face returned to its calm, grim mode.

"That doctor fooled you."

"What?"

"He knows ain't no one know where that grave is. No one you can talk to, at least."

"What do you mean?"

"Only one man knows, and you can't go to him."

"Why not?"

"Because he don't talk to white folks. His people don't. And you can't go where these people live."

"Why not?"

"They live like the old days, like the old country. Only one man knows where Sorry George is, and that man is a witchdoctor."

"I've met a witchdoctor already."

Petruchio raised his eyebrows.

"No, son. This ain't what you met. His daddy's daddy came on the boat. He does things the old way. A real witchdoctor. Not a root worker like Crow."

"I will go see him. I came this far, and I'm not afraid."

Gretel put a hand to her mouth and smiled.

"Reminds me of you, Petruchio."

The dark man leaned against the railing and showed his teeth in a half-grimace, half-grin.

"That ain't a good way to be," he said.

"You had your chances along the way. Give him his," she whispered.

"It's not mine to give." He looked at Minnow. "I can tell you the way, but the way is yours."

Minnow nodded.

"They live in a forest village. Near a road. It don't go the whole way, but it can get you close."

"Can you show me?"

"Like I said, I can show you. But it's your road."

"Will it be safe for me?"

Petruchio put a hand to his chin and rubbed his stubble.

"No telling what's out on the islands. What's out on them roads. No one can tell you if you'll be safe. It's your road."

"But the road is there."

"It's a road, and it should be a quiet road."

"I can walk a quiet road."

"You watch out on them quiet roads, and hope if a noise comes, it comes from a living thing."

Minnow thought of the warning that the hunters had given him. The things in the woods. The haints.

"Yessir."

At that moment the storyteller must have finished, because the porch erupted in applause and hoots and calls for another tale. Minnow licked his lips and looked at Petruchio, who had tilted his head down to light a cigarette. He looked at Gretel, who had turned back in the direction of the storyteller. He looked for the dog but did not see it. He rubbed his stomach and then put his hand to his eye. Nothing too bad, just a little pain, some blurriness.

"I'll take you to the road in the morning. Rest good and I'll show you the way."

"Thank you."

Gretel smiled at him.

"Go listen to the next story, Minnow. I'll show you a bed when you're ready."

A woman told a story about a ghost that lived in the sea. Varn and the gang would have liked it.

BED WAS A HAMMOCK BETWEEN TWO palmetto trees, slung in the strip of woods between the beach and the village.

Other hammocks were occupied, some were empty. Candles glowed in open shacks built on the tree line, with people bedded down under little roofs, right on the beach. People remained near the porches, milling around, talking quietly. The group dwindled, though, and folks left on the path to the village, or up the beach, or down the beach. Only a few torches still sent their glow out, and the world went quiet.

Minnow rocked in the hammock, pushed by the cool breeze. He tried to think of his father, of his mother, and of how many days he had been gone. Of what they might think of him as the guest of honor up on the porches. He tried to think of what he might find on the quiet road to Sorry George's grave. But then he slept.

He woke only once, swaying in the breeze that came from the ocean, over the river. Cory stood next to the hammock with one hand on its edge, arm moving limp with the gentle rocking. Gretel stood over him, carefully cleaning his cheek. She put a finger to her lips, and Cory left when he saw that Minnow was awake. Minnow fell back asleep to the sound of the waves, smelling the sweet perfume of Gretel's skin and clothes, like flowers.

MINNOW WOKE UP IN THE hammock with his stomach full, legs rested, body warm. The waves brought a peaceful hush from the beach, and the breeze cooled him in the trees. The porches were empty, silent. The beach was abandoned except for a few smoldering torches. Only the slightest morning sounds came from the village, just past the trees behind him.

He put his legs over the edge and stood up almost on top

of the dog. He stood next to the animal and crouched down to rub its head. The dog chewed on a busted crab claw, trying to find some morsel of meat inside. Minnow stretched and rubbed his own full belly and stared at the dazzling light that burned on the wide river through the trees. He walked to the beach path and stood looking out at the sparkling water, alive, living. He winked his right eye and could barely feel any pain at all. The cuts on his face had scabbed, and felt better now.

He went to the village with the dog and stood before the fire. Gretel came first, standing silently next to him. They watched the coals glow for a moment without moving. Gretel gave him a new pair of shoes: old leather soles patched with sweetgrass thongs. Minnow took them and examined the careful, tight weaving. Done by someone's hands, right in the village.

"Thank you."

"These shoes will help you walk free from trouble. But you got to help them, too. Stay out of trouble, little boy."

He put the shoes down and stepped into them, wiggling his toes to set the thongs. A bruise on his left foot complained, but he could barely feel the other scrapes that he had gotten since losing his old shoes.

"They feel good."

She rubbed Minnow's hair.

"Thank you for everything. For the food. For helping my eye."

"I hope you find what you're looking for."

"Me too."

"Remember us when you get back to town. We'll still be out here, even when you're done."

"I will."

Gretel left, and soon Petruchio came from the beach,

silhouetted by the sparkling water as he came down the path. He wore his hat tilted low and carried a big bag around his shoulder. Cory followed behind him, wearing nothing but his short pants. Petruchio dropped his pack and stooped down to check its contents.

"You're leaving," Cory said. A statement, not a question.

"It's time for me to go."

"I hope you find what you need, out there."

"I will."

Cory looked at the fire, then at Minnow.

"Never made a friend from town."

"You have one, now," Minnow said. "Maybe I will come see you again sometime."

Cory smiled, but Minnow wasn't sure if the boy believed him.

Petruchio finished tying his bag closed and hefted it up to his shoulder.

"Let's go."

They went out of the village on one of the many paths that led out into the jungle. They passed the last of the shacks, storage houses, and animal pens. The trees took over, thick and hot around them.

"The graveyard you lookin' for is in Coffin's Point. I couldn't tell you which one."

Coffin's Point was a big plantation out on one of the larger islands beyond Frogmore. Minnow knew that much. It was owned by white men but worked and inhabited now by freed negroes. A whole hamlet had grown around the Big House: complete with cemeteries, stables, barns, fields of cotton, and wide open rice flats.

"Won't matter even if I could tell you which one. No way you gonna find the grave without finding someone who knows it."

"And that's why I'm going where I'm going."

"And that's why you going where you going."

"Yessir."

Minnow glanced back and could not see the village. He saw only trees and vines and bushes, and movement where the dog followed them, picking through the underbrush. Soon they came to a sunny clearing where the path broke into three directions.

"You gonna have to be careful as you go on. The place you going is old. The place you going isn't like the place you come from."

Minnow nodded and asked, "Which way?"

One path widened almost into a road, and it looked freshly graded. It had shallow ditches on either side and was flanked by live oaks the whole way. Petruchio pointed down that way.

"That's the way to Coffin's Point. Not your way right now." Then he pointed to a path that led off to the south. "That way goes off to the river you came in on, way off." That left only the third branch, which was barely a rut in the woods. Looking down, he could hardly see a path at all. Maybe it was just a game trail, low and winding. The dog approached it and sniffed the verge.

"That's your way."

Minnow tilted his head and looked at the woods. A gust of wind blew in from over them and swayed the trees and flattened the grass. A cool gust. Something different. Then it was gone. Petruchio turned his eyes to the sky, squinted, and then looked down.

"How far will I have to go?" Minnow asked.

"You gonna follow this trail through the woods a while.

Cross two creeks. Then keep going as the woods change."

"Two creeks?"

"They small. You'll have to get across some way. That's how it is."

"What then?"

"The woods will change, and you'll come to a place where the path breaks off into two. There'll be a jumping horse there."

"Jumping?"

"Yes he will be. You take a right at that path, follow the little road all the way down. You'll find it there, or they'll find you."

"What if the horse isn't there? What if I miss the branch?"

"He'll be there," Petruchio said, laughing.

"Thank you for everything," Minnow said. "I don't know what would have happened if you hadn't found me."

"I'm just helping someone who needs help. Walk fast, now, or dark will come before you get there."

"Thank you again."

Petruchio patted him on the back and sent him down the path. Minnow looked back once and waved, then turned and sped up along his way. The trees fell away on both sides, leaving no canopy and only a slot of clear blue sky overhead. Butterflies and grasshoppers fled the grass at his approach. The dog stayed well behind, hidden in the tall weeds.

They pushed on and crossed both creeks. The first one was dry, and the second one was narrow enough that he could jump it, and the dog could too. If Petruchio had thought those creeks would slow them down, he hadn't thought of the water they had crossed to get as far as the village.

They followed the narrow path, warmed by the sun. His cheek hurt, but making progress on the path made it hurt less. The dog moved ahead as the grass grew shorter, setting a faster pace.

They went around a bend, and a creek came up beside them, bordered by marsh. They walked close to the marsh, smelling the mud, smelling the salt water. The creek went on into the distance, and Minnow could see where it opened into a river and a sound, with a hint of the ocean beyond. Two boats were out on the sound, arrayed with fishing gear. The men on the boats were just narrow shadow shapes to him. One of the boats was motionless in the water, but the other was moving fast without oars or sails to power it. Minnow stopped and squinted and saw two thick lines leading into the dark water, taut. Something was pulling the boat, and he thought it might be a ray. His father had told him fishermen would race boats on the water, sometimes, when they hooked the big rays.

They kept walking, and the trail led away from the water. Minnow was growing tired and out of breath by the time the path widened and took them back into the woods. He called for the dog to slow down, and it did.

The island changed as they moved away from the water. The palmettos dwindled. The underbrush thinned, and they walked through a forest of skinny oaks. Pine trees grew tall amidst the oaks, like sentinels. Every so often they would pass a live oak, growing alone and colossal, spreading its long spidery arms over a vast piece of forest. They went on, and the trees grew tall and close together, making a shady canopy over a dim wood. The path turned to a narrow road: flat, gray, littered with leaves. Minnow saw no sign of any traveler, and the whole forest was silent except for his footfalls.

They reached a place where the dusty road branched in two directions. The horse was there, as Petruchio had said it would be, and now Minnow understood.

They approached it slowly, with the dog making a wide circle around the tree. The tree was a live oak, still young. Its trunk was gnarly and thick, bigger than two people could put arms around, with bark rough like chunky granite. The trunk doubled halfway up, and slung between the gap was a horse skeleton. It was bones, sinew, and even some skin, all white and dry like a mummy. The bones of the hind legs and rump stuck through one side, and the neck and fore-legs hung from the other. The ancient crackled mummy lay draped through the tree, quiet and still.

The dog sniffed the air. Minnow got closer and examined the sparse cobweb hairs that still protruded from the horse's shriveled back. It had a mummy mane, torn and balding, but the rest of it was dry-rotted skin, bare and rough.

"How do you think it got there?" he asked, but the dog just whined.

Minnow went a little closer and smelled the dusty, petri-fied skin. It looked soapy and gray, stretched taut over the old bones. He went around the tree to the other side and examined the yellowed teeth protruding from a bleating skeleton mouth. He stared into the empty eye sockets, at the sharp rims of bone. He put his hand out, with two fin-gers extended.

A bird called out, a nasty crow call, and Minnow jumped. He rubbed his neck and looked at the dog.

"This is where we turn."

They left the jumping horse and followed the little road. Now and then he thought he heard the sound of hoof-beats.

A SWAMP BLOCKED THE WAY. It wasn't a marsh. It was closed in. Stagnant fresh water stood in deep, dark pools. Twisted oak saplings and stunted pines grew all around, clutched to the few patches of high ground that rose from the murky water. Bright green pond weed floated in a flat, verdant carpet, hiding wide swaths of the surface. No bridge offered a way across, just the road ending abruptly before the swamp. The whole world seemed gray and dim, and the sun—now dropping from its highest point—was held back by the tangled canopy.

Minnow's legs ached, and he almost fell to his knees. Petruchio had said nothing of a swamp. They'd come the right way. They'd turned at the jumping horse. Minnow rubbed his eyes, taking care to avoid rubbing the inside of his right eye. When he looked back up, a gray shape slipped down into the water twenty feet in front of him: a flat gray shape, long, noiselessly submerged.

He looked at the dog and it looked at him, then back at the swamp.

"You see that?"

He stepped away a few steps, but the dog stayed put. A ripple came from farther out. The dog growled.

"Come back some."

The dog stayed where it was. It watched a crow fly across the water just in front of them, almost skimming the surface. Nothing else moved.

Minnow licked his lips and looked left, into dense brambles. He looked right, down the swamp's tree-pressed water line. The trees grew right up to the edge, leaving just a sliver of gray, algae-coated mud between water and wood.

The crow called out from nearby. Another bird answered, but its call stopped short. Minnow looked up. The whole swamp had gone quiet.

The swamp was not that large. If he followed the water's edge in one direction or the other—through the brambles or along the tree line—there might be a place to cross farther down. Maybe the road was still there, waiting for him to pick it up on the other side. From his place on the bank he could see only a mess of mud and brush far across the water.

The dog hadn't moved its stare.

"Which way do you want?"

He could find almost no way to go along the tree line to his right. He'd have to have one foot in the water and one foot in the trees. But the brambles were no better. Twisted bushes of thorny vines and ivy spiraled along the wider bank on his left. Even if he could stay out of the water, he'd be moving slowly. He'd be tangled up, and he'd be helpless.

Minnow rubbed his eyes again. The scab near his right eye ached when he touched it.

A splash, and a bird screaming, then silence. The dog barked. Not a fierce barking, but a solid warning directed at something out in the water. The dog backed up with each bark, scooting until it was right next to Minnow. It whimpered, barked once more, and then circled in place. Its tail wagged and went straight, then it stood there, looking over the dark morass.

"You think you found a gator? Has to be a gator."

But the gray thing had been big. Just the part he'd seen had been as big as a big gator.

"Pick a way."

The dog didn't move.

"Then I'll pick it for us."

He went to the right, to the thin line of mud along the trees. The water seemed shallow enough along the edge, with just enough room for him to walk. He tiptoed along the bank of mud, at first. He expected the ground to be more slippery, but his sandals caught the surface and he was able to walk the mucky line between water and trees. He kept his left foot out at the water's edge by pressing close to the woods, using his right hand to grab trunks and vines as he moved along. He could see the muddy swamp bottom for just a foot or so, and then it dropped off into darkness. The dog picked along behind him, able to stay closer to the trees and farther from the water than Minnow.

Minnow kept one eye out on the swamp. It was still and quiet, except where bugs broke the surface and left fleeting ripples. The dark, deep rhythm of frog croaks came to them from far away, hidden all around in the woods. They moved, stopped. Moved, stopped. Each time they stopped they would look over the water.

The dog saw it first. It straightened its tail, and the hair on the ridge of his back spiked up as it did when they fought the boar a few islands earlier. The dog growled deep, mean, unlike any sound Minnow had heard it make before. When Minnow looked, he saw it too: the hint of a shape in the water, long, submerged. Maybe just a shadow in the mud, maybe an ancient tree fallen and waterlogged. Then it moved.

"Let's go faster," Minnow said, and he slipped on the next step, splashing his foot into the water as he scrambled ahead. He cut his eyes to the left and saw the shape moving more quickly, parallel to the shore, still far away, but speeding up.

He walked now with one foot in the tree line and the other tiptoeing through the edge of the water, each step made clumsy by the slimy mud on the bottom. The dog seemed to follow suit, staying against the ragged tree line as much as possible, stepping in the water only when the passage along the edge was blocked.

Minnow glanced back and the shape was gone, but a slight wake of ripples betrayed where it had gone under.

They moved faster, as fast as they could, and then came to a place where the trees pushed out like a wall of spikes over the water. There was no way under or over, and no way into the dense woods. Minnow glanced over his shoulder, at the way they'd come, and then looked back at the obstacle in front of them.

"Come on," he whispered, and they abandoned the muddy edge.

He led the dog around the clump of trees that had grown out into the murk, staying in the shallow part where he could still see the gray mud beneath the tea-colored water. They were all the way in it, ankle-deep, the mud sucking at his sandals. He used his right hand to pull himself along by branches and scrawny trunks. They rounded the protruding barrier and he looked out over the swamp from the horn.

The thing was floating there. Its entire top side was exposed: gray, gnarly, ancient. Its body was wider than a bateau, and—though its snout was pointed right at Minnow—he could see the monster was longer than three tall men together. Both eye ridges showed, but the one on the right was a gray, puckered socket. The plates on its back were long and spiked, and many of them were broken and hooked and scarred.

Then it submerged.

"Come on," Minnow said, flat, quiet. He was moving already, rounding the barrier that had pushed them away from the shore, into the swampy water. "Come on," he urged.

They came around the other side of the obstacle and got back to the bank. They splashed ahead full force now, unworried about noise or movement, tearing along the edge between water and woods. Minnow scrambled down to his knees, got up to his feet, then ran as best he could in the rancid water.

He looked back and saw the thing. It had surfaced again, and it had made up two-thirds of the distance between them. It swam on top of the water now, quickly closing the remaining space. He saw one red eye set in the good socket, burning like a ruby. The thing stopped, sliding to a halt not ten feet behind them, and opened its maw to hiss. Steam and smoke billowed from its gaping mouth and from its nostrils, curling in black tendrils through the heavy swamp air. It chomped down, gnashing finger-long teeth that were yellow and jagged. The beast launched itself forward, and the dog bounded out into the open water to avoid being eaten. It splashed into the swamp, and started swimming across.

Minnow flew forward along the bank, frantically splashing away from the thing and the dog. The edge of mud broadened, and he could now run out of the water, but the thing would be right behind him already. He was dead. His feet hit solid ground and he looked back and the monster had hesitated, watching both boy and dog. It chose the dog and slid soundlessly away from the bank to pursue the animal. Minnow forced himself to look away, to make good the sacrifice that had been made for him.

The mud bank melted away, and he was back in the water. He stumbled on, but then heard a bigger splash and a violent thrashing behind him. He looked over his shoulder and saw only gray skin and churning water and waves breaking as in a hurricane. The thing hissed again, and the swamp hung heavy with smoke and fumes.

Minnow slapped his hand at his left pocket. Not there. He felt his right pocket and almost lost his balance. He stabbed his hand in and pulled the pouch free. Still running, he undid the leather drawstring and pulled the flask out. His wet fingers fumbled, and the heavy glass vial tumbled through the air, flipping twice before he caught it just over the surface of the water.

He looked back and the thing was gone. Minnow did not stop. He jammed the leather pouch into his pocket and ran through the shallows. He was at his top speed again just as he saw the shape coming at him. The ripples raced across the surface, faster than should have been possible—coming as if someone had sped up the entire world except for him. He made one last dash along the water's edge, and his legs gave out.

He heard it first. The low moan and the hiss that came with the spreading of the awful jaws. Then he felt the breath, and smelled the sulfur gas belched forth from its yellow throat. He whipped around and there it was, almost walking on top of the water, lunging at him. Minnow pulled the cork free with his teeth and threw the flask out, vial and potion together, spilling the fluid on his fingers as he let go. He screamed, his heart stopped, and the bottle shattered against the thing's nose. It reared its head, unfazed, and glass bits popped off its thick armor like harmless pebbles. Minnow swallowed and closed his eyes, but the end never came. He looked again and saw the thing thrashing in the water. Bubbles and steam and blood roiled off the monster's skin wherever the potion had touched.

The beast reared its snout up again and made a final lunge, but Minnow had not wasted the time won by the potion. He was two lengths away from the thing now, and it could not close the distance fast enough. It stopped again after the last lurch, hissing and blowing off steam and sulfur. The potion was still working, and each place where the drops had splattered—including a hand-sized spread across its awful head—had turned black and charred. It squirmed and flailed in the mud, then lunged again, this time a shorter distance. It lashed its head and caught a trunk as thick around as a baseball bat in its jaws, then uprooted it and threw it out into the swamp like a twig. Minnow left the creature behind, tearing at the forest and thrashing in the mud and the water. It bellowed as he escaped.

Minnow ran. He rounded a curve in the water's edge and fell forward onto solid ground. He flipped himself over onto his back and scrambled away from the water, watching the edge for any sign that the thing might come with new strength to devour him on dry ground.

He jumped to his feet and did not slow down when he found the road. He ran until his heart ached and his lungs burned. Then he collapsed in the dirt, watching back down the path for any sign of the gray monster.

Minnow sat there, watching the path, listening to the forest. A few birds chirped, and the wind moved the high canopy. He breathed heavily and let the air dry him while the sky overheard began to grow darker. The falling sun alarmed him, as the forest was not a bright place to begin with. It would be darker still at night. With the dog gone, it might be the darkest, yet.

His heart kept drumming, beating hard from the chase. His body trembled, and he shivered at the thought of the monster. And the boar. Two monsters so far, and other dangers. The rivers, the jungles. He had never planned on this. It should have been a simple trip, but it had become so much more. There would be more monsters, if he went on. The next one might kill him. That would be worse than returning with no medicine. Not returning at all.

He could turn back, he knew, if he was careful to avoid the swamp and the beast in the water. He could retrace his steps, get back to the village. Gretel could help him find a way home. And he could see Cory again, and the quiet little beach where they'd held the long feast. His mother would be so happy to see him.

But that would not help his father, who was helpless now in bed. Minnow sucked in a stuttering sob and licked his lips, turning to look ahead, farther into the jungle. His path was not the easy way. He nodded and got to his feet. He brushed off his dirty clothes and checked his pockets. Then he thought of the dog.

He looked back and hoped to see it, but his confidence faded. The dog had never left him for long, and it should have returned by now. But it hadn't. He wanted to cry. His eyes went wet. His breath went ragged, into sobs, but he clenched his teeth and tried to stop. He wiped his eyes and smelled whiskey on his fingers.

He turned ahead to face a narrow winding path through the woods, gray, leaf-strewn.

"I hope you're eating something good, somewhere."

He walked the path alone. It closed around him, and his arms brushed branches and leaves as he slipped between two walls of green forest. The sun was setting, making the hints of sky turn pink and yellow and orange. He smiled when he saw it, but when he looked back down, his path was as dark as ever, and it made his heart feel the same.

He had walked the forest road in Frogmore at night. He'd found trouble then, too, and now he thought about the horrible monster in the swamp. That ancient, gray beast that had come at him like some demon in the forest. Its red eye, its fuming mouth. The noises he had heard as the dog was caught.

He stopped and listened, heard nothing, and walked on as night fell around him.

The moon rose in the dark sky, offering meager silver light. Only crickets kept him company, screeching their thin song out through the forest. His eyes adjusted to the dark, and he found himself walking through a dark wood under a black slot of open air. All he could see was the sandy gray path just in front of him and the trees creeping ever closer. The warm air smelled green and fresh, like after a long rain, or before one.

Miles later the crickets stopped. He froze in the path. He knew what that silence meant. He knew that someone, or something, was nearby. Then he heard the new sound. The sound was in the air, running all through the woods, thumping deep in his chest, but coming straight down the path. Drums. A strange rhythm, an old song.

"I hear you out there," Minnow spoke.

But he did not move right away. He listened. He listened, maybe trying to hear some instruction or clue in the music. He needed the people playing the drums. The tattoo of their secret song would bring him to their place. He had to go there, but he didn't want to. Petruchio had warned him that they would not be like anyone he'd known or met. They would be like from old times in Africa. His body felt cold, and a phantom finger ran up along his spine.

He swallowed and walked on, then sped up, almost jogging, running toward the sound of the drums.

They got louder, filling the air, filling his ears, his head, his heart. Many drums: deep low drums that beat in slow rhythm, hard-sounding drums that brought a faster song, and light airy drums that sounded like heavy bells adding a melody to the dizzying music. Drumming filled the world, but it rang sharpest just ahead, just down the path. He followed that sharp call, passing side paths and forks along the way, watching the night, following the sound of the drums.

He walked through the music until he felt a hand touch his shoulder, this time flesh and blood. He saw it out of the corner of his eye, even in the dark: a slender black hand, ebony almost, the long arm, and then the whole man emerging from the shadows. His face was hidden by the night. He wore ragged gray pantaloons cinched with a sweetgrass belt. He was naked otherwise, glistening with sweat. His eyes were wide, white, with piercing dark holes at the centers.

Minnow froze in place, and the drums seemed to fade. A second man emerged from the woods and stood at Minnow's side, and a third man came from behind them. All of them were black as pitch, only eyes and teeth showing in the dark. Their mouths moved and they spoke a strange language. He saw flashes of white as they spoke.

He pulled gently away from the hand, but it held him firm.

"Please let me go."

More talking, and the drums went on.

"I'm not here to bother anyone. I'm looking for someone."

One of the men, behind them, came around and appraised Minnow and said something to the others. He shrugged, then put his hands up and walked away, shaking his head.

Minnow felt the grip tighten on his arm, and one of the men shook him and turned him so that they were eye-to-eye. The man grimaced, showing his teeth, and then nodded at the other man, over Minnow's shoulder. He released his grip and gave Minnow a push, a push back down the way he'd come. Both men closed in on him, waving their hands as if to shoo him away. They spoke fast in their strange language, fast and angry.

"Please."

They pushed him again, down the trail. The drums got louder.

"My name is Minnow."

The man who'd been walking away stopped and turned to face the three of them again.

"What did you say?" He walked back up to Minnow. His accent was thick, with each syllable coming quick and clipped off his lips. He sounded like the negroes in Port Royal who traveled on boats from the Caribbean.

"My name is Minnow."

The man's first words had been curt, maybe even a little angry. But when Minnow said his name the second time the man cocked his head and then smiled.

"Like the fish?"

Minnow nodded, and the grip on his shoulder relaxed. The man on the left laughed.

"Well then," the man in front of him said. "We got something for you."

"You came," another man said. "Just like Grayeyes said."

"Grayeyes?"

"He told it a month ago. You was coming."

Minnow staggered and put a hand against the side of his head. A dull aching built there, inside his skull.

"A month? How—"

But the man held up his hand to stop him.

"Don't think, don't talk. Just come."

Minnow followed the man down the path with the other two following. One of them melted away into the forest, and the leading man dropped back to Minnow's side. They walked into the sound of the drums, and Minnow's head pounded with each beat.

They passed through a small village of huts, all built from palmetto fronds and pine logs and straw. Fires burned in clearings and at places where paths met. The whole world seemed empty of people, except for them. No women, no men, no dogs, no children. Just Minnow and his escorts walking along the snaking path, past dark huts and empty log benches and low-burning fires in sand pits. The drum beats came from ahead, farther into the village, farther along the path.

"Where are we going?"

"To the hall," the man said.

"What's there?"

"Everyone. Everything."

They quickly crossed the village, which was smaller than Gretel's village, as far as he could see in the dark. They followed the path around a cluster of huts, and he saw the hall. It was a tall, wide structure built of logs and fronds and straw. The front had double doors, like a barn, and the roof rose to a steep point above. The two great pine timbers that made up the main corner supports were carved with animal figures and painted red and black and white. All of the drum music came from in the hall: the cacophony of beating, and now clapping, and now foot-stomping as they came closer. One voice rose over the sound, yelling and calling and singing in some strange tongue.

The path turned sandy white, lined on each side by clay pots burning with flickering oil flames. The white sand led right up to the closed doors.

"This way."

They led him up the path, and his heart beat faster and harder with each step he took. He couldn't look around anymore. His eyes were frozen on the doors, which were also carved with figures: panels of reliefs showing faces, people, more animals. They were frozen there in scenes cut by some deft hand. Bizarre eyes, long tongues, two-headed beasts, ocean waves breaking against dunes.

He blinked, and the hall was still there. It was the hall he'd come so far to find. The hall he'd sought, the hall that might hold the secret of Sorry George's grave. He'd come so far, and now they were leading him up the path. A golden light shined through a crack beneath the two doors, and from there wafted the smell of sweet perfume and strange, pungent smoke. One of the men stepped ahead and put his hand on the door's handle: a wooden knob carved in the shape of a wild pig. The man pulled the handle and opened the right-hand door, revealing the scene within.

The clay pots led on, lining an open dirt aisle that went from the doors to the far end of the hall, where a strange altar stood. The altar was adorned with all manner of painted wood carvings, canvas tapestries, stick men, sculptures decorated with bird feathers and pine boughs, animals carved from stone, wax candles of all heights and colors. More carvings hung from the ceiling on strings: twisted figures of animals, painted things, whiskers of wire, eyes of glass.

People were gathered on either side of the aisle, behind the burning pots, a mass of women and men, children and infants, dancing and beating their feet against the dirt floor. The drums were behind them, near the walls, and he could see people moving to take turns at them, continuing the relentless rhythm without pause. Big drums, small drums, racks of drums, drums that hung from the ceiling and drums that people held in their arms. The dancing continued and the music did not stop. They seemed unaware that he was there.

The men moved him through the door, and the smell of incense washed over him, mixed with the musty odor of sweat and skin and oil. He stumbled, and the room spun around him, but the men held him up and kept him on his feet. Someone closed the door, and he stood there between his escorts, looking up the path toward the altar. Then he saw the man at the front of the room, dancing.

His was the voice Minnow had heard, a voice that rose in a shrill song over the drums. A voice that led the drums. He had to be the witchdoctor, dressed in pants sewn from a patchwork rainbow of dyed fabrics, bare-chested, wearing some strange carved mask that made his head appear to be a mix of a lion and a bird. Feathers and bristly fur stuck out from the mask, which was painted in colors to match his billowing pants. He struck both his arms out in front of him as his feet moved, and he brought them up in a wide arc over his head—pointing to Minnow, looking at Minnow. He did not stop singing, did not stop dancing.

The men took him up the aisle, slowly, walking on either side, and the people in the crowd took notice. They didn't stop their movements, but they turned to face him as they danced. Some directed their motions at him: flapping hands, arms slinking like snakes, bodies twisting and thrusting. When he was halfway to the altar, people started to call out. They joined the witchdoctor's song with their own voices, and the drums played harder to match.

"What's happening?" Minnow asked.

"They calling for you."

His escorts didn't speak again, and instead took him all the way up to the altar, right before the witchdoctor himself. The tall, masked man leapt down from the dirt platform on which he danced and circled Minnow, bending down to level his colorful mask with the boy's face.

The mask was strange, but not scary. Minnow stood his ground while the two men backed away and the witchdoctor circled him, appraising him, looking at him with round gray eyes through the holes in the mask. While he did, Minnow felt the music grow inside him. The drums that led him, the drums that kept him, the tattoo of feet and hands and clapping, the ringing of voices in the long smoky hall. He closed his eyes and felt his heart beat with that strange music.

Then the noise stopped. It stopped as if sheared off by a razor, as if blocked out by a lead curtain. Minnow opened his eyes and the witchdoctor had his arms up. The drums were silent, with only their ringing in Minnow's ears as proof they'd ever played. The people were quiet, and the dancing had stopped. Now they swayed back and forth, some of them interlocking their arms. The children rocked to and fro, and some of them held their hands toward the ceiling. Minnow swallowed and looked up at the masked man. Every eye in the hall was on them.

"The fish who would swim to us on the hard river. The fish that heard our music." The witchdoctor's voice was booming, deep, like someone speaking inside of an empty barrel. His accent was thick.

Minnow nodded and tried to find a word to say. He stared at the altar and at the witchdoctor and opened his mouth. His tongue felt dry, bloated between his lips. His forehead beaded with sweat.

"I've come for your help."

And the whole place erupted in conversation and discussion. People talked and gestured with their hands and made faces like they spoke of something important and interesting. The discussion faded, and only a few children kept whispering when the witchdoctor spoke again.

"You come for help?"

Minnow nodded.

The witchdoctor's hands passed across the altar and stopped over a scattered collection of tokens. They were small: fabric squares, paper packets bound with twine, cloth scraps folded and sealed with wax. Each one looked full, packed with unknown ingredients. Roots. The witchdoctor picked one up.

"You need love?"

Minnow shook his head.

The witchdoctor put the first root down and picked up another: just a twisted knot of string wound around something. He waved it in front of Minnow's face, and Minnow smelled something dusty and foul.

"Luck?"

Minnow didn't answer. The witchdoctor knew he hadn't come for a charm, or a curse, or any other root that another root doctor on the island might make.

The witchdoctor waited. He let the crowd begin to murmur, and then he held his hand up again to quiet them.

"We know what you come for. You come to find something. You come over river and field. Through marsh and swamp. You seen many a thing that make you scared. You scared now?"

Minnow looked around at the people, at the hall, at the altar and the doctor.

"No sir. Just a little out of place."

More conversation in the crowd, this time shorter, and then quiet. The witchdoctor cocked his head.

"You know what you really here for?"

Minnow did not move.

"You come here to die."

Minnow stepped away, but his escorts were still there, both men standing like statues. The witchdoctor stayed frozen, too, but a new man emerged from the group and clapped his hands and spoke in that strange language. Conversation broke out in the crowd again. People began to leave through the front doors. Some left from side entrances near the altar. The candles and torches flickered with the drafts of their movement, and swirls of incense smoke moved in ragged clouds overhead. Many of them cast their eyes on Minnow as they left, looking curiously at the little boy standing in their hall.

The witchdoctor remained motionless, as if frozen in a tableau after delivering his last words. A few of the children lingered, then finally trailed out. A cat went with them.

The doors closed and they were alone in the hall: Minnow and the witchdoctor. The torch flames righted into long, thin columns, and the candle flames burned smooth and tall around the altar. Incense burning at the walls and among the abandoned drums sent wispy coils into the air. The place glowed orange, dim but not dark, with shadows filling the rafters and jumping against the walls.

The witchdoctor moved like a shadow, fluid like ink as he went to the altar. He removed his mask and showed a normal face, dark skin, short hair. Except for the eyes: milky white, unseeing.

"I'm not afraid of you."

Grayeyes smiled.

He set the mask down on the altar and it became just another strange thing among so many other strange things. The noise of the crowd outside faded, and soon everything was quiet except for the soft sputter of the torches. Minnow wondered if anyone was left outside, anyone who could try to stop him. He wondered if the doors were locked. He wasn't too near the witchdoctor, and he wasn't too far from the doors.

"You come all the way from town," the witchdoctor said, turning to face him again from the altar. He knelt down so his eyes were level with Minnow's. His teeth were bright white, his skin clear and young. He was not an old man, like Crow.

"Yes."

"Then you must not be scared. You come a long way."

Minnow nodded and clenched his teeth. The pressure on his jaw made the side of his head ache. A tear squeezed from his right eye, and it stung where it came out.

"My father is sick and the only thing that can help him is in Port Royal. Doctor Crow sent me for dirt off of Sorry George's grave."

The witchdoctor's cloudy eyes opened wider at the name.

"I was told that you know where it is," Minnow said. "I need the dirt as price for the medicine."

"So that's most of it, is it?" the witchdoctor asked.

"Most of it, yes."

"For you especially. But you ain't done yet."

Minnow shook his head. "No. I'm not here to die."

Grayeyes turned his head left, then right, as if to get a better look at the boy who stood in front of him.

"Sorry George is in the graveyard on Coffin's Point. The one at the end of the avenue. They call it Brickyard, last I heard. Maybe they still do. Got a wall around it made of red bricks. Tall. With wrought iron gates. That's where you got to go."

"I knew it was in Coffin's Point."

"Now you know right where it's at. If you can't find the exact spot where he is, all would be for nothing."

Minnow nodded. "That's why I came to you. Can you tell me?"

"Yes. But you got a choice to make."

"What choice?"

"I told you. You came here to die."

Minnow glanced at one of the side doors, which were closer to him. The witchdoctor saw him and moved between him and the way out.

"You got to make the choice: do you want to live, or you want to die."

"I just want to find the grave."

"Then you in trouble. I'll tell you the spot right now, but if you walk out, you as good as dead by the time a few days pass. Only grave you'll find is your own."

"Why?"

"You don't know?"

Minnow shook his head and felt the dull ache. But now the pain was more acute. He could feel where it was. The place where the branch had stabbed him. The place where he'd bled and lost his sight, and where the thick scab had plugged the hole. He put his hand up to the swollen flesh and almost fell over from the pain.

"You got the rot behind that eye."

"No," Minnow said.

"You won't make it clear of the swamp like this."

"No," Minnow said, and took his hand away from his face.

"His grave is under the only live oak tree in that cemetery. His grave is right up at the trunk. Kids play on it all the time and don't know. Look at all that green moss that grows around the trunk, and you'll find something, maybe. You'll know it."

"Thank you. Thank you so much."

"You go out down the same road you came, but you'll see another path out around the swamp this time. Don't mess with that plateye no more, else you make him mad enough to come up here, and then I have to deal with it."

"Thank you."

"You can thank me now, but you get on that road to Brickyard and you'll only be thanking God for welcoming you up there to him."

Minnow glanced over his shoulder at the door. He put his hand in his pocket and felt the pouch, ready for the cold grave dirt. Then he put his hand back up to his eye. When he pressed down it hurt, and he felt it weeping something hot.

"It hurts inside already," the witchdoctor said. "This is your choice."

Minnow nodded. His head spun, from the smoke and the heat of the candles, and from looking into those gray eyes.

"We was afraid you wouldn't hear us. Wouldn't get here soon enough."

Minnow took a step back.

"I can still walk."

He felt sick from the pain, and the perfume in the air made him feel sicker. The pain behind his eye went from dull to sharp, a precise stabbing that inched deeper and deeper, like a worm burrowing into his brain. Maybe into the part that made him Minnow. He stumbled to his knees.

"Can you help me?"

"I can help you, but it's going to cost."

"I don't have anything to pay with."

"Sacrifice, Minnow. You ain't gonna be the same when you wake up."

Minnow tried to lift his head, but when he did his vision spun in the wounded eye and he thought he would retch.

"Help me. Please."

He put both his hands on his stomach and heaved a dry cough. When he sat up straight again two men were standing alongside Grayeyes. They lifted him by the shoulders and then one carried him like a tiny doll in his massive arms. The witchdoctor led them into a shadowy room behind the altar. A room lit only by candles.

The two men stayed with them after putting Minnow on a cold wooden table. The witchdoctor moved around the room from shelf to shelf, searching and then retrieving, looking and then nodding or muttering to himself. One of the men began a soft murmuring, maybe a prayer, in the fast-rolling tongue. It was like dark, rich music. The second man lit a stick of incense, and the fragrant smoke put the room in a haze, thicker over their heads where it swirled like a gray fog.

Minnow moaned and tried to put his hand to his eye, but the man lighting the incense gently moved his hand to his side. Someone put a warm blanket on him, and the witchdoctor came with a small wooden bowl cupped in his hands.

"Drink this."

"What is it?" Minnow whispered.

"It will help you dream good dreams."

"What is it?"

"Drink."

Minnow took the cup and drank the clear liquid. It tasted like warm milk and left grit on his teeth. The second man wiped his face with a rough cloth and then poured something over the skin, letting it run down all over his face and his cheek. It tingled where it ran over on the wounded eye.

"Be calm."

The witchdoctor came back wearing a helmet of polished steel, domed at the top, with a guard over his nose and flat protections over his ears.

"Blood tonight," he whispered. "The last man who wore this took blood from the people who lived here first. Killed them and raped them. He wore it until his head came off and then his bones wore the helmet until it came to me. We are not far from times of blood."

Minnow tried to focus on the intricate etchings on the helmet, but his vision was blurry in both eyes.

"Be calm."

The last thing he saw was a long wooden instrument in the witchdoctor's hands: ebony maybe, black as night, sharp like a needle, polished like tortoise shell and catching the candlelight, like magic.

He saw their little house. The grass looked dry and dead in the summer sun. His father lay inside: a long white shape under a gray and tattered sheet. Only a pale pink face showed, framed by ash-colored hair. Lips dry. His mother stood nearby, hands clasped. The dog was in the dream, but not at the house. It was in the woods somewhere. Deep in the woods. He saw a bent old negro walking toward him down a narrow gray road, drawing closer with each slow step.

✳

HE WOKE UP. The candles were burned to waxy stumps. The incense had stopped fuming, but a light haze still filled the room. The room was quiet, smoky, musty. Musty like old dust long settled. Only a little golden light shined from under the crack in the door. He was staring at the slender line of light when he realized he could not see out of his right eye.

His hand fell on a soft square of leather. The leather was held in place by a strip of fabric lashed around his head and behind his right ear. A spongy piece of cloth was folded beneath the patch, and it felt like some sort of poultice was packed beneath that. The hole where his eye should have been felt cool but throbbed with a dull, steady pain. He moved, and the pain did not flare.

His fingers stayed on the patch, pushed in a little, and he felt the absence of the eyeball to match the absence of sight. There was no dark where his vision should have been, no black. Just nothing. He could not focus on anything in the shadowy room, and when he tried to look around he felt like he was flailing a paralyzed limb that he could not feel, or use, or sense. He covered his other eye, and then rubbed his free hand through his greasy, tangled hair. What would his mother think if she saw him: one eye, maimed, an incomplete boy. In a witchdoctor's closet. Tears welled in his good eye. What would happen if he cried?

"You will not die now."

Grayeyes stood with his arms folded across his chest, a dark shadow in the dim room.

"Not from the eye, at least," he said, and a white smile spread through the shadow of his face. He walked close and appraised the patch. He cupped Minnow's face in his hands.

His palms were soft and warm. He tilted Minnow's head and peered into his remaining eye.

"How did you do this? You're not a doctor," Minnow said, his voice dry and raspy.

"Not the new way. Only our way saved you. Don't forget."

Minnow nodded.

"It was your sacrifice."

"I know."

"You will make it to the cemetery safe. It's the same road you came in on. It will take you to the avenue. Won't be hard to find it from there."

"Why did they bury him there? Why not out here?"

"Nobody wanted him when he died, he was so sorry. But he had to be hidden. So they didn't bury him with his family, or with nobody he knew, or anywhere anyone knew. They took him out to old Brickyard and put him under a big live oak way in the back, away from all the other graves. Maybe graves are there, now. Maybe they dug him up without knowing and mixed some old white man up with his bones."

He laughed loud in the little room and clapped his hands once. Then he rubbed them.

"I ain't been there in a long time."

"Why did they hide him?" Minnow asked.

Grayeyes took one last look at his face, peering close at the patch. Then he stood up and moved for the door. He turned to Minnow and pointed at him.

"They hid him because of people like you."

✳

GRAYEYES TOOK HIM FROM the medicine room, through the empty hall, to the open doors. The world had changed.

The sky overhead was gray, cast with wispy black clouds that swept through the air on a high wind. The full strength of the wind did not reach them below, but a steady breeze worked the forest into whispers. Now and then a gust would blow down, shaking branches and sending wooden chimes to clanking. The village was waking up under the overcast sky: children playing, dogs stirring, men rushing away down paths. All eyes were on the sky.

Minnow sucked in a breath of air: cool from the night and the breeze, fresh and salty.

"A storm is coming," Grayeyes said.

Minnow nodded, without pain. The eye that had hurt him was gone, and his mind no longer burned and ached with fever. He shook his head gently and felt fine.

"You can go now, and try to finish what you've begun."

"I don't have any way to repay you."

"You paid your price already."

"Will I succeed?"

"I do not know. But you got a lot in front of you. You have come through the darkness into night, but it's still out there waiting for you. You can see it better, you know?"

Grayeyes turned to him and stared into his one good eye. He put his index finger on Minnow's forehead and nodded.

"Sometimes when we lose something, we find another thing to take its place."

Grayeyes took his finger down and gazed out over the village. Campfire smoke reached them on the breeze, rich and scented with cooking meat.

"Break your fast with us, Minnow, and I will send you with a guide to Brickyard."

Minnow ate breakfast: grits with butter and salt, corn on the cob roasted on coals. Goat's milk and cream. He felt full and ready for the road. A young woman wrapped dry grit cakes in greased paper and gave it to him to carry on his way.

Grayeyes summoned a tall man dressed only in loose white pants and gave him instructions that Minnow could not understand. Grayeyes put his hand on Minnow's shoulder and appraised the patch, again.

"Goodbye, little fish."

The guide led him away from the village. The road was familiar, and the guide showed Minnow a way around the swamp that kept them far from the black water. The guide would walk only so far, though, and when they reached the jumping horse he refused to go farther. He indicated a path with his long, skinny arm.

"That way to Coffin's Point. That way to Brickyard."

Minnow took the path west, away from the horse, following it until it widened and packed down into a gray dirt road that would lead him to Sorry George.

HE WALKED THROUGH THE MORNING and crossed a wide road that ran north and south. He stopped in the middle of it and looked for people but saw only one solitary figure walking far to the south. The sky had gotten darker as he walked and was messy with long gray clouds. He squinted and tried to see the person down the road, but in the dim light he could not make out any details. That way looked good and would lead him home, but he turned back to the other path.

Minnow left the intersection and followed his path to a causeway across a wide marsh. The pathway came out of the trees, and the earth dropped away into a broad marsh basin, full of water on a high tide. The path went ahead, across the marsh, on a raised bed that left two feet of dry pathway above the water. The water was up high, but he could still see the tops of the marsh grass, and he could see where winding creeks would make a maze on a lower tide. Trees circled the enclosed water, and the only notable feature to be seen was the dark place where the causeway led back into the forest on the far side. The steady wind was a quiet hush against his ears. His hair blew in it, and the water lapped at the causeway as he crossed.

Live oaks flanked the avenue that led to the old plantation and to Brickyard. The trees might have been three hundred years old, with trunks so big that four men could not have circled them. Their bark was thick and chunky with deep channels. The oaks had grown tall and spread their long limbs in an arcing canopy over the path. Moss hung down from the branches all along the way. The spiraling tendrils drifted to and fro in the wind, except when gusts blew and whipped them into tangles. Leaves rustled, and the longer branches bounced in the wind, but the solid trunks remained motionless.

He walked the avenue, passing empty fields broken by stretches of forest. He ate the grit cakes for lunch and threw the paper in a ditch. He passed a shed, an old abandoned stable, signs of an often-used camp. He went by a few shanties and one log cabin. Then the graveyards. They were old things, grown over, borderless, only one of them still closed in by the remnants of an old wire fence. Brickyard would be farther, closer to the heart of the plantation. He passed the cemeteries carefully, with a hand on his pockets. He saw no people, but he found the dog again, at the last one.

A gray shape darted between the faded, leaning stones. At first he thought it was another ghost, a haint, a plateye.

Maybe one of Sorry George's dangers coming at him to slow him on his way, or stop him entirely. He left the road and crossed a brick border that might once have been a wall. The dog was there, sitting next to a tall granite stone. The thin marker stood like a stone wafer, solid in the ground. The dog cocked its head and licked its chest and then looked at Minnow.

"Are you the same dog?"

The dog stood and joined him. Minnow didn't touch it, but it followed him back to the avenue. He rubbed its head, then brought his hand up and adjusted the band on his eye patch. The place where the witchdoctor had worked felt good, but the world was cut in half to him, and it was not easy to understand. They went on their way.

A great white mansion stood at the end of the avenue. It would have been the Big House, once, and was probably still the heart of the plantation. The house towered high: three floors, a red roof. Each story had a porch with white columns, white rails, and white rail posts. Two big stone staircases curved up to the front door. Wide fields surrounded the manor, and a river lay behind it, leading out to another sound. The avenue ended there, and smaller roads led off on either side. Minnow could see a brick wall farther down on the right. It had to be the cemetery.

A few people toiled over a piece of equipment in the far corner of a field. A cat walked across the front lawn, and seagulls glided over the Big House roof, riding a rough wind that blew in from the ocean. Their sharp calls came to them, standing at the crossroads.

Minnow led the dog toward the brick wall. The Big House went by on their left, revealing more of the river and the sound behind it. The ocean was out there, wide and limitless, with no land to close it in or hold it back. The sky over the house was gray, and the cloudless horizon beyond was a matching dull white. The high clouds made a slate-colored ceiling, swirling and passing overhead on the wind. Two children came from the Big House, around from the back. They saw Minnow and the dog and ran off.

The road narrowed as it took them to the red brick wall. The wall stood almost twice Minnow's height, with velvety green moss growing over the rough brick faces. A black wrought-iron gate was built at the middle of the wall, closed. He could see gravestones on the other side, gray and leaning. He went up to the gate, examining the hammered scrollwork, and swung one side open. It creaked so loudly that he thought the gang might hear it back at the hideout. He waited, listened, and then slipped through the gap.

A brick path wound through the cemetery. Different plots were marked by low iron fences, or brick borders, or by neat rows of small smooth rocks. A few even had their own brick walls, chest-high to Minnow. Many of the graves were aboveground crypts, white stone boxes big enough for a single coffin and a single corpse. The ground was too wet, too low, so the bodies were laid to rest on the surface, with the living. Minnow felt cold as he passed by dressed skeletons and rotting coffins, kept away from the world only by thin crypt walls.

The biggest crypts were brick, large enough to hold entire families, built like low houses with no windows. Each one had a square of newer brick where they had been opened and reopened over the years. One of them had a half-crumbled wall, and Minnow could see cobwebs and shadows inside when he passed. He wanted to look inside, but felt bad just thinking it. He found a small chapel with windows and doors boarded up, and even a makeshift shelter built of sticks and vines where mourners might seek cover in bad weather.

He walked the brick pathways, twisting his way past family plots. Some were well-tended, clear, with headstones almost new. Other plots were overgrown with tall grass and scattered with leaves. The stones were leaning, broken, or missing. The oldest graves were just patches of dirt, no name, no marker.

He walked, and the wind shook the canopy over his head. Pine needles fell around him, and clumps of moss broke free in the harder gusts. Leaves rattled along the walkway and the dog chased them. The whole place was quiet except for the wind and the dog's quick steps.

He read names, some familiar from town, some he'd never heard. He stopped to look at the newest stones, and the oldest, and walked around one of the larger crypts. He put his hands out to feel the soft moss that grew on the ancient bricks, and at that moment a sharp blast of wind cut through the graveyard, rattling wrought iron, blowing streamers of moss overhead. A twisted limb broke from its place and fell, cracking over a tombstone with a sound like thunder. He withdrew his hand and looked down at the dog, crowding in close against his sandaled feet.

"We can't waste time."

He looked across the graveyard toward the back and could see the rear wall through rows of stones and monuments and crypts. A tree was there, a single tree, alone, away from all the others.

"George," he whispered.

They went down the path to the back of the graveyard. The tree was strange, like a live oak in size and shape: broad trunk, spidery arms, thick bark. The bark was rough, like the armor on all live oaks, but this tree was almost gray. In some places it appeared silver, as if a silky web had been laid over its skin. A live oak's dark glossy leaves never turned color, but this tree's leaves were burnt red, deep and rich like clay from the earth. The plots had dwindled, leaving an open spread of land beneath and around the tree. A few ancient stones were leaning here and there, but everything was overgrown with tall grass and wiry weeds. The tree stood alone, almost against the rear wall.

Minnow approached the tree, and the dog sniffed around under the shade of its canopy. The branches swayed in the wind, and the shadows beneath the tree moved and changed with each moment. Gray clouds swept across a fading sky. The day was still young, but darkness fell all around. He reached up, touched one of the branches, and picked a red leaf. The dog returned to him.

"Find anything?"

They walked under the shadow of the tree, looking at the ground. The dog sniffed at piles of leaves, and Minnow kicked at any notable rock. He went back and forth in tight rows, scanning his eye over every inch of the dirt under the tree.

"Nothing," he told the dog, who'd gone off to leave his mark on the crumbling remnants of a marker. "Stop that."

The dog came back, and on his way he paused where the shadow of the branches began. The weeds stopped there, hindered in growth by the shade of the canopy. The dog circled a few times, then put his nose to the ground and snuffled.

"What is it?"

Minnow left his place next to the trunk and joined the dog at the perimeter of the canopy. He dropped to his knees and brushed away pine needles and crumpled leaves to reach the solid layer beneath. The dog scratched at an adjacent piece of dirt. Minnow squinted, rubbing his hands around the spot, feeling.

Something was there. Smooth, domed. When he brushed more dirt away, he saw it was as big as his stretched palm, etched with horizontal growth lines.

"Conch shell."

He began to dig under the edge to pry up the shell, then stopped. The dog watched him and the shell.

He left the shell and brushed away more leaves. Nothing. He made another clear spot off in the other direction and found the second shell. Just like the first: set into the ground with only the very top showing like the dome of a skull. He dug around and found the other two. Four in all, marking the corners of a grave. Even if the ground had been clear, the shells would have been barely visible in the dirt.

Branches stirred overhead, moving constantly now in a steady wind. Thunder rumbled in the distance, heralding wispy clouds that flew across the angry sky. The sun was hidden completely, just a white blur behind the gray. Leaves and moss spiraled around the graveyard in dusty wind devils, and Minnow smelled salt on the air.

He looked down at the grave.

"Sorry George," he said, "my name is Minnow, and I've come a long way to find you. You've sent me some trouble as I've come. But I don't know you, and you don't know me. All I know right now is that I need your help, and you're gonna help."

The limbs overhead groaned. The wind blew the moss into a fury, tangling in every branch and limb. The wind sheared in over the high brick walls and made a long howling noise. Minnow clenched his fists.

"I've come a long way," he said, raising his voice over the wind. "And all I need is something that you're not gonna miss."

He knelt down on the ground in front of the grave.

"Doctor Crow said you'd send three things. I believe the plateye was one," he said, digging his hand into the cold dirt, scraping up the hard topsoil into a dark pile. "And I think this storm is the next."

He fished in his pocket and took out the empty leather pouch and opened it. The dog whimpered behind him.

"But maybe those convicts were yours too. Or maybe that boar. Had to be that boar. That means if I get through this storm, I'm done."

He scraped the dirt into the pouch, as much as he could, packed it, and cinched the leather cord. He held the pouch out over the grave. "But I think between what I've had coming out here, and what I'll get going back in…we're even. You and me."

He covered up the hole with leaves and pine straw. Wind rustled through the tree as he brushed a final layer over the disturbed plot. He studied the sky, gone from gray to near black. The whole world looked dim and gray, and the wind felt sharp and wild.

He turned back to the grave, hidden again. Nobody would know it, unless they knew where to search. He thought about his gang. He thought about the hideout, and about being downtown. Leaving the first day. Port Royal, and the ferry. Leaving Newfort under a blue sky. Everything in between. Now all he had to do was get back. He had to cross all that water and get back to Dr. Crow. He could get home, and one day he'd have a good story to tell in the hideout.

But first the storm. They had to find shelter, or all the goofer dust in the world would not matter.

"We have to go," he told the dog, but hesitated.

He felt in his pockets and took out the leather cup.

"I got this from another ghost," he whispered. "You can have it. A gift from me."

He unfolded the little cup and put his quarter into it. He kept his last dime. Minnow bent over and put the cup on the covered grave.

"It's all I can give you."

They fled through the tombstones, and the wind blew at their faces, as if to hold them back. The sky continued to darken, and the once-distant thunder boomed over the plantation. He'd been out in storms before. He'd braved thunder and the lightning. But this was different.

They reached the gate and found it closed, sealed by an ancient lock. Minnow looked left and right and confirmed that it was the same gate they'd come in through. The lock was clamped at the middle of the gate, holding the doors closed. He took it in his hand, old and rusty, unlikely to allow a key even if he had one. He abandoned the gate and walked along the wall, slowly at first, then faster, trotting with the dog at his heels. The wall was in good shape and still standing tall. It was wider at the foot, with no adornment at the top to trouble his climb.

He found a place where a patch of bricks had broken away from the interior, leaving a shallow foothold. He tried it but could not reach the top. Another gust came over them, blowing his hair and sending the dog into circles. Minnow ran now, to the end of the wall, scanning with his eye as he went, finding no footholds. He turned the inside corner and went along the far right wall that bordered an empty wooded lot. Minnow found another place where he could put a foot, and this time he discovered a second hold that he could climb to. From there he could reach a spindly branch that hung over the top of the wall. He jumped from his hold and grabbed the branch, dangling for a second before he kicked up the rest of the way and hauled himself over. He dropped down the other side, ran back to the gate, and called the dog. It came to him, spurred on by a crack of thunder. It shimmied under the gate, and they were reunited outside the cemetery with goofer dust in hand.

They fled down the side road back toward the Big House. The wind came steadily now, blowing through the woods and across the fields and over the river. Whitecaps swarmed on the water, and Minnow could hear breakers crashing in the distance whenever the howling wind settled. He saw no birds. No sun. The sky was gray, and the world was set in false twilight as he approached the Big House. Real night would be coming soon. The day had left him.

"We have to get out of the storm," he told the dog.

They needed a place to shelter until the weather passed. They might have to stay overnight, even, though it would mean delaying the journey home. The black clouds roiling overhead were not going to offer a gentle rain. After the storm they could go. They could leave Coffin's Point for the road that would take them to the ferry and to Dr. Crow. But first, shelter from the storm.

He considered the Big House, but he saw no light inside. They passed a few outbuildings, a shed, and what appeared to be old slave quarters half-tumbled to the earth.

The dog trotted ahead, leading the way down the road past the Big House. They turned on the avenue of oaks and the dog led him into a run. He checked the goofer dust in his pocket and then sprinted, his sandals slapping against the hardpan down the middle of the road. The wind whipped at them as they left the protection of the live oaks, and he put a hand to his eye patch as a spiral of dust blew over them. They left the avenue and arrived back at the causeway, but it was covered with water.

He looked down, down along the causeway he'd come in on, and saw only water. The tide had been high when they had crossed, but now it looked like another tide had come in on top of it. The creek-riddled marsh had become an open expanse of gray water, churning in the wind. The whole flooded plain was surrounded by woods, but the wind was still hard enough to drive the high water into choppy waves. Minnow stood on the bank overlooking the flooded causeway, and he felt what the storm really was.

He glanced over his shoulder. The Big House was way down the avenue, barely visible. The live oaks stood strong, but their branches were swaying and bouncing in the wind.

"We have to get up high."

The dog went back and circled one of the closest trees, but Minnow shook his head.

He looked down the avenue, to the woods. They'd seen shacks, barns, sheds. Maybe something to climb.

"Come on."

They raced back down the avenue, looking left and right through the bordering oaks. Not a barn, not a shed. Not high enough. They were halfway to the Big House, but the road looked long and the air down that way was more open, the river closer. He stopped and put his hands on his knees, then looked into the woods. Left was no good: dense trees, one road off in the trees, and an old tumbledown house. To his right the trees were sparser, and he could see something—a building—way off in the woods.

"Come on," he said, but the dog was already following as he slipped through two live oaks, jumped a ditch, and ran out into an open meadow.

They entered more woods on the other side and found the slightest respite from the wind. Minnow picked his way through, passing an old horse trough and a piece of rusted machinery. A house was ahead with some sort of corral and a shed. They smashed through the last few trees and stumbled into a clearing. Minnow ducked his head to protect his face from one last branch, and when he looked up he was almost on top of a little colored boy. The boy stood at the edge of the trees, dressed just in short pants.

The door of the shack-house burst open and a woman stepped out.

"Bo! Bo! Get in here!" Her dress whipped in the wind and her voice strained to beat the howling gale.

The little boy ran away from Minnow and the dog and took shelter under a live oak on the other side of ther yard. The oak was bigger than any of the trees on the avenue. Bigger than any tree Minnow had ever seen. The dog followed the boy, and Minnow went after them and joined them under the tree.

"Bo!"

The boy pointed at the woman.

"That's my mama," he said.

"Who's that?" the woman called.

"She says a storm is on us."

"She's right," Minnow said.

"Who is that?" she yelled.

Minnow looked down at the boy, back up at the woman, and raised his hand.

"Ma'am!"

He kept his hand up as a salute, and walked toward the house, stumbling when a particularly strong gust caught him broadside. The little boy followed with the dog.

"Who are you?" the woman called loudly, even as they stepped close. She put a hand on him before he could realize what was happening and pulled him into the house. She flung him in on the floor and waved the boy and the dog in next. The wind whistled at the door, and she slammed it closed.

"This your dog?"

"Yes ma'am."

"Then he can stay."

The house was dark. Minnow turned onto his back and then got to his feet. The woman cracked the door and peeked out into the storm again.

"Storm's here."

"Yes ma'am."

"You looking for shelter."

"Yes, but—"

"Where did you come from?"

She turned back into the room. Beautiful smooth skin, dark in the shadows, wrapped in a rough, white nightgown. Her boy came to her and hugged her leg. The wind howled outside. Whatever final heart the day had was fading, leaving only the dimmest light to come in through chinks in the walls. The house shuddered with each gust. It creaked and shifted.

"I came from Newfort. Downtown. I'm going back there, but the storm came in."

The woman looked around the room, at the ceiling, at the walls.

"You think it will pass?" she asked.

Minnow shook his head.

"No ma'am."

"What kind of storm is this?"

"The water is rising. The causeway is covered."

She snapped her head at him. The boy whimpered at her leg, but the dog nuzzled his hand and he got quiet.

"Is anyone else in the house?" Minnow asked.

She shook her head.

"We can't stay here."

She put her hand to her mouth. Maybe as if she were fainting, maybe a gasp, maybe a laugh.

"Are you crazy? This the best place we can be. Right in these walls."

Minnow slid his teeth together and looked at the dog, the boy. He thought about the causeway and how close they were to the river and the sound.

"The water is rising," he said. "We may ride out the wind, but the water will carry everything away." He clenched his fists as he spoke, like he could will her to believe.

She shook her head and then bent down to pick up her boy. He was almost too big to hold, but she managed. Minnow looked at the door and wondered if they could all run back to the Big House. This was not the storm he'd imagined when he had left the graveyard. This was something else, and it was howling alive outside.

"We have to get up high."

"I ain't got no attic. Roof can't hold us."

"Not in the wind. We have to use the live oak."

That time she swooned, rocking, and Minnow moved to break the child's fall, if nothing else. But she kept her feet down and her head up, even on the verge of tears. The light outside was gone, and he could barely see her features in the dark.

"This whole place is going to be washed away," he said.

With those words, the wind seemed to drop into a lull. Rain began to fall, tapping on the roof, thudding on the dry ground outside. A bolt of lightning showed gold light through every crack in the house. Thunder followed.

"We won't be safe out there," she said, but Minnow could tell she understood.

"Do you have any rope?"

"Out in the shed."

Minnow nodded and gathered up the dog. The woman squeezed her boy.

"Can you climb?" Minnow asked, already knowing the answer. The boy was years younger than Minnow, but he'd be a climber. The boy nodded and buried his face in his mother's breasts.

"Go out and put him up in the tree," Minnow said. "You go up after him, and I'll bring the rope."

The woman nodded and licked her lips. The four of them looked at the door, and Minnow opened it.

Night had fallen, and the world was black. They saw no lights in the distance, no torches or candles or lamps bearing any hope. The far-off wind sounded like the ocean. The sound hypnotized him, but then a wave of wind roared over the house and the stinging rain brought him to attention. He couldn't see anything but the black oily shine of wet leaves. And the live oak. Its outermost branches whipped with the wind, but its interior limbs only rocked gently within the protection of the tree's canopy. The trunk was like a pillar of stone in the earth, unmoving, unaware of the mounting storm.

He stepped out first and braced himself against the gusts. The hardest ones forced him to reset his feet, but he could stand and walk between the blasts. Minnow took a few steps into the stinging rain and looked back. A slicing gust of wind shook the house, and that was enough to send the woman out with her boy.

"Go on!" he yelled, leaning into the wind.

They ran for the shadow of the live oak, and he ran for the shed. The dog kicked in his arms and twisted its body, so Minnow let it jump down to the ground out in front. It kept its head low, tucked its tail, and led Minnow to the shed. Minnow threw open the door and the dog slipped into the edge of the threshold for shelter. He tore through the shelves and knocked over a bucket and a stack of cut lumber. Then he found the rope. Two coils.

"You staying or going?"

They both looked out at the world through the narrow shed door. The rain blew sideways through the darkness, and all Minnow could hear was wind, wind, wind.

He ran, not even checking to see if the dog followed. Halfway to the tree the top of a barrel blew by, turning end over end like a quarter flipped from a thumb. He put one hand over his patch and ducked into the live oak's reach.

The world beneath the canopy was only a bit calmer, but it was shelter enough to catch a breath, check the dog, and secure the rope. Then he heard them crying. Minnow circled the tree and found the cleft in the trunk where the two biggest limbs branched away. He looked up and saw the woman straddling a branch, with her boy under her, pressed into the bark.

"I'm coming!"

He took the dog first and set it up in the deep cleft at the crown of the trunk, just over his head. If it had leapt out or gotten scared, that would have been it. But it cowered down and stayed tight in the cleft. He hauled himself up next, kicking up against the rough bark, climbing a few feet into the space with the dog. It squirmed under his weight, but he stood and started up one of the limbs that branched from the trunk's crown. He went on the limb next to the woman's, scooting with his legs straddling each side. His feet dangled, and his sandals flapped in the wind.

"I don't know if I can hold on!" the woman yelled. They were almost within arm's reach on the two different branches, but the ripping gale carried her voice away.

Minnow leaned in and squeezed his branch. He pressed his cheek against the cold wet bark and closed his eye. The branch was solid and thick, but its size made it hard to get his arms around.

"Take this," he said, sitting back up and holding out one length of rope. "Put it around you and the branch."

The woman leaned up and the boy cried as he was exposed to the open wind. She said something to him, leaned over, and took the rope from Minnow.

That's when he heard the crash, and the rushing. The dog began barking below them in the cleft. The rushing sound got louder, like a mountain river torn into rapids.

The woman lashed the rope around her back and then swung one end around the tree. She did it the first try, and

Minnow looked at his rope and wondered if he could do the same. But her rope wouldn't wrap around far enough to tie. She was stuck, leaned in with one hand on the loose end, and the other end across her back. It wouldn't go around both of them and still tie at the ends.

Minnow looked at his rope. Same length. A gust caught him and he almost fell off. One skinnier limb was under him, twisting off like a spider's leg, and beneath that was the ground. Only the ground wasn't there anymore. The rushing sound came louder, and he knew what had happened. The water had risen from the sea and flooded the world. He felt dizzy, and looked back at the woman. She was looking at him already, and he knew what she knew.

"Take mine!" he yelled, holding out the second coil. "Tie yourselves together, to the branch!"

He could see the bright smile through the night, the woman shaking her head. She dared to bring one hand to her face to wipe off a slick of rain.

"No, boy."

"Take it," Minnow said, holding it out farther.

The woman drew in her rope, and this time lashed it only around the boy, then around the limb. She tied it with three knots, and then leaned in on top of him, hugging tight.

The rushing sound grew louder, and now a crash came as the shed collapsed and broke in the torrents like thunder.

"Best tie yourself, and not let it go to waste. I'm sure you got a mama would want you to come back sometime. Just like me and my baby."

He thought of his mother, of his father. Both still waiting. Waiting back home. Waiting in the very same storm, maybe. He looked across the gap at the dark woman. She was a shadow in the night, hugging her boy against the limb. Minnow lashed the rope around his waist, around the limb, and then knotted it. He squeezed the knot in both hands.

The water had risen halfway up the trunk, a foot short of the cleft and the dog. The dog whimpered and pressed itself against the tree. The water rushed and ripped and showed gray foam where debris swirled in its torrents. The whole island would have to be under water.

The hot summer wind did not feel so hot after he was soaked. The ragged gusts broke over his face and his body, forcing his eye closed, blowing against every inch of his skin, eyelashes, hair. The randomness of the buffeting wind made it terrifying. Just when he thought he was used to the wind it would rush in like a steaming train, howling and blowing, salty on his lips, tearing at his clothes and his hair.

Then came another explosion of sound. A ripping noise, then a whistling sound as wind filled the little house. Crashing and smashing as the contents broke and flew away. The walls next, crunching and tearing. A final rocking boom as the entire thing collapsed into the flood. Nothing to see. Blackness beyond, just the black bowl of the tree, ragged and wild in the night wind. The woman screamed, and her boy cried. The water flowed beneath them like a vast black river, parted by the solid trunk.

The wind came in full force: sustained, blasting the tree, bending even the stout limbs of the live oak. The weakest limbs snapped. The canopy's bowl offered no shelter from the gusts, and now the rain strengthened. The stinging spray became a drenching downpour that flew at them sideways. Thunder clapped and lightning flashed, and for just that second he could see every leaf and twig on the tree. The wind came swirling under the branches and carved waves that broke against the trunk. The wind hammered down. He squeezed himself against the branch. He pressed his face against the cold, wet limb. The dog howled. Minnow looked up along the length of his branch, then out into the darkness beyond. He looked back to his left, at the branch next to him, and the woman was gone. The storm did not relent. The noise, the power, the cold rain. He squeezed his eye shut again, and felt hot tears behind the lid.

A STOOPED OLD NEGRO with white hair laughed at him. He could see it with both eyes. The man's back was bent and he slapped his knee with each laugh. He wore purple sunglasses. When he stood up straight he stopped laughing and stared right at Minnow. His face was solid, unmoving, angry. The dog barked and woke him up.

The roaring darkness had left the world, and the sun rose to send the night away.

Their tree stood fine. Its branches were stripped of leaves, and most of the outer limbs were snapped. One main arm had splintered and cracked, but the trunk and the tree stood unmoved. Minnow had squeezed his branch all night, all through the darkness. He felt a part of it.

The boy was still tied to the other branch. He was motionless, limp, and alone. The rope had done its job: the boy appeared unhurt, and Minnow could see his chest moving with breath.

Minnow peeled himself off the branch and felt his pocket for the goofer dust. It had been soaked, turned to mud, and now remained as a damp clump. He'd kept his sandals, and his clothes were fine except for the soaking. He listened for anything. No birds. No dogs barking. He looked for his dog. The flood had receded and left a muddy floor below, strewn with debris. A body lay naked under the tree. It wasn't the woman. It was a man with a big belly. He had gray-purple skin, and his face was turned down. The corpse blended in with the trashed lumber, tree limbs, and bricks.

Minnow felt his rope and started working at the soaked knot. He did it without looking, while he scanned the ground below for signs of his dog. He untied himself, checked the boy again, and then backed down his branch.

He climbed into the empty cleft and again surveyed the ground below. The remains of a dock appeared to have broken around the tree and snagged there even as the black rapids had finally receded. The man was tangled in the dock wreckage, bloating in the morning sun. Minnow adjusted his patch and checked the poultice underneath. It was damp, but felt fine. He made a final check of the tree from the cleft, as a sailor would check a boat after a bad storm. Still solid. Still safe. Battered, but still safe. He looked down at the wasted ground below, took a breath, and jumped.

Minnow hit the ground clear of the wreckage, as far from the body as he could have hoped to land. But the corpse was still close, wedged under a massive piling. Its legs were twisted on one side, and its torso stuck out the other. Where its head should have been there was only a ragged neck stump. The frayed edges were dark and black, and something purplish coiled out of the top.

He lurched forward, put his hands on his knees, and vomited. His eye watered, and he even felt a strange sensation where his other eye used to be. Like he was crying, but nothing was coming out. A tingling. He rubbed his good eye and stood up.

"Is he dead?"

The boy had woken up on the branch. Minnow looked up and the boy was actually upright, straddling the limb, hands planted in front of him for support.

"Yes," Minnow said. His voice came out a dry scratchy croak. He swallowed.

"Who is it?" the boy asked.

"I don't know."

The boy hitched at the rope and searched for the knot.

"Where's my mama?"

Minnow looked back at the dead man, and then gazed out over the countryside. The flood had stripped the world bare. Patches of trees were left, here and there, and a few live oaks were still standing, but the trunks of smaller trees were scattered like toothpicks. The tidal surge had wiped everything away. Houses, woods, roads. The land was strewn with debris and junk and trash and bodies. His eye wandered from a toppled chimney to a cracked boat hull to the remains of an old water tower. Broken lumber, dead cows, human bodies. The bodies were muddy and twisted and at first hard to see in the chaos the storm had left behind. When Minnow looked closer, he saw them everywhere. Under a fallen trunk. Protruding from a mound of lumber. One man was draped over the railing of a steamer left stranded on its side.

"I don't see her."

Minnow checked his sandals, caked with mud. The ground was thick with black mud. Everything was covered in it.

"Help me."

Minnow looked up and thought about the boy's mother, about where she really was. The rope had held her boy. He was safe.

He went back up the tree, into the cleft, and untied the boy. He helped him down the branch, and the boy jumped when he was ready. They stood under the live oak amidst the rubble. The dock lumber. The dead man that the boy could not take his eyes from. Minnow heard something first, something digging behind them, then the boy noticed too. They both turned, and there was the dog. The boy stumbled backward, almost falling over a splintered tree branch, but Minnow grabbed him by the shoulder and stood him up.

"That's my dog."

The boy nodded and wiped his face with his hand, though it did no good against smears of mud and a scabby scratch across his cheek.

The dog came up, and Minnow patted him, looking back and forth at the dog and the boy until the boy patted him too. The boy knelt down to rub the dog's ears, and Minnow looked out over the dead bodies again. Hidden unless you really tried to see. But once you saw them splayed out under the morning sun, you couldn't miss them.

"You have any family around here?" Minnow asked. The question was a stupid one, maybe. Everyone out on the islands was related. But maybe they were all bodies now. Dead bodies like the ones scattered all around.

"Yeah," the boy said. "My auntie and uncle live down past the Big House. My other uncle lives out in the woods."

Minnow looked across the direction he'd come, toward the avenue. The live oaks were out there, still standing, and a bare strip that used to be the road. The land was a patchwork of ragged woods and piles of rubble, but most of the world was washed flat and empty. He couldn't see far enough in the other direction to spot the Big House. It would probably be gone, anyway.

"We better go," Minnow said.

The boy looked around. He looked at the dock wreck. If the body there bothered him, he didn't show it. He turned to where his house had stood.

"What about my house? What about my mama?"

Minnow shook his head.

"Maybe we can find your aunt or your uncle. Let's go."

They went to the road with the dog out in front. It seemed to sense the bodies. Minnow would see one coming and the dog would lead them around in a long path. It delayed their trek, and Minnow knew the boy was seeing all of the corpses, but they did their best to stay as far away as possible.

They passed through the line of oaks, onto the road, now just a muddy trench between the trees. A body was there, face down, planted deep enough that it was almost covered. It was naked, and the skin was scoured raw and pink. The boy cried.

"Come on."

Minnow was convinced that the entire island had died, but then they met another living person at the end of the road where the way narrowed to a sodden path. The man was thin, old, with gray hair. His clothes were dry, though, and he seemed unhurt.

"That's Rudy," the boy said as they approached.

"You know him?"

The boy nodded, and when they got close he ran up and hugged the man. The man put his long skeletal fingers on the back of the boy's head and mumbled in the strange island speech that Minnow could not follow. When the boy turned back he was crying. The old man held a hand out toward Minnow.

"He says thanks for bringing me safe."

Minnow took the gray hand and shook it. He looked into the old man's eyes and nodded. The two left Minnow and the dog at the edge of the path that led through the wind-stricken woods. He watched them go up along the avenue, back toward the Big House, leaning together like two thin sticks.

THE CAUSEWAY WAS GONE EXCEPT for a narrow band of raised mud and scattered bricks that crossed the dry marsh. The tide was low, the surge gone, and the landscape had changed. Every channel was wider, every creek bigger. The cuts were deeper, and the woods that surrounded the field were blown sparse. He could see a far horizon that had once been hidden by trees. His hand went to the dog's head.

"We can cross this easy."

They started down the muddy path. The storm had churned the pluff mud, and the breeze brought a musty sweetness to his nose. It reminded him of playing on Bay Street, in another life, and made him feel strong under the morning sun. The dog perked its nose, too. The path was scattered with bricks and rocks and aggregate laid down over many years. The foundation had failed in some spots, and they had to hop across short gaps or slog through the mud at longer ones.

He heard the moans halfway across. At first he thought an animal was trapped in the mud, but then he saw the creature was a person. The man was buried in the pluff mud neck deep, with a little bit of shoulder and one arm poking out. His head was smashed on one side and the hole appeared to be packed with mud. His skin was coated, slick and gray. The arm wobbled in the air, and his mouth moved with each gasping moan, but Minnow saw no sign of fight. No struggle.

Then another. He saw the leg and the arm first, just one leg and one arm protruding from the mud. They were shaking in sharp lightning movements, jerking up and down. Farther on another person was buried waist deep, clawing at the mud with one arm while the other hung limp, broken backward at the shoulder. That person was coughing up blood, too. Cries filled the air, weeping, moaning, gagging. Wounded and maimed people were buried and stuck everywhere, some writhing in pain, some barely moving. For every living soul dozens of bodies were scattered around the muddy field like battered dolls.

The man with his head bashed in was still alive, though. He was there, stuck in the mud, just a hundred feet off. The next closest people were farther out, trapped in a deep creek bed. He might not be able to reach them, but the man was closer.

Minnow looked along the causeway. Bricks. Mud. He found a snapped pine branch and pulled it free. The dog started barking. The moans got louder at the barking, and more of the bodies came alive. The arm and the leg protruding from the mud began shaking violently. They knew he was there.

"Be quiet," he said to the dog.

Minnow stepped down the causeway's ruined bank and slipped. His butt hit the bricks and a lightning pain shot up his back. He caught himself with both hands, bit his lip, and stood up. He found purchase on the bricks with his sandals and took a breath. He was smeared in mud by the time he reached the bottom. He used his stick for balance, and tried to judge the distance to the groaning man.

"Hello!" he yelled.

The man did not respond. The leg and the arm quit moving. He looked back up at the dog, down the causeway. No people, but buzzards wheeling high in the air. Probably a hundred of them. The broad black wings caught thermals and the birds turned in graceful clockwork circles, high, just black angles against the unbroken blue.

The man's head rolled on his neck, and he moaned again. The dog whimpered. Minnow had mud-bogged before. He and his friends bogged for fun, bogged for oysters, bogged for treasure. He could try and get to the man, try to help pry him out. He took a step, and his leg plunged into the mud. He lost his balance and fell forward, but he managed to get his other leg out and wound up sticking into the mud with his legs instead of his entire body. He was up to his waist, almost, and he trembled with the realization that he was now in the same position as the dying people. In the same mud. It wasn't like normal pluff mud. This had been churned and whipped and it didn't even give the slightest resistance. You could sink in pluff mud, but this slurry was worse, like whipped cream.

Minnow took a deep breath. He moved a little and sank more, but he did not panic. He pushed himself forward through the mud and dug with his arms. He pulled his legs backward, lifting them up through the mud, and made swimming motions. He put the stick out front, held between both hands, and raked himself up and out of the hole.

The suction held him, actually pulled him back, but he had been in mud before. He was careful, and his sandals stayed on.

Once he was flat on the mud he tried crawling. Usually he could crawl along the surface, but now the mud was too soft and he was sinking. He breathed carefully, keeping his lungs full of air as if to float on water.

He made slow progress, crawling past lost pilings and scattered planks. He went by half a shingled roof that cast a shadow on him as he swam across the top of the mud. He passed a corpse, bloated and smelly. He could not count how many he'd seen so far. He could not stop to think.

The man's head kept rolling as Minnow shimmied closer with his stick out front. Minnow could only spare enough breath to whisper one word.

"Hello."

The man did not react, and Minnow pressed on through the mud. He was almost close enough to reach the man with the stick. The man's entire body was coated with pluff mud, and in some places the mud hung thick in globs that showed periwinkles and marsh grass roots. The open place on his head was dark with clotted blood and packed with mud.

"Hello?"

The man sprang to life, his arm stiffening and his head jarring upright. One eye opened, smeared with gray. The man screamed, and waved the arm, and got the stick in his hand. He pulled harder than Minnow could have imagined, pulling for survival and strengthened by fear. Minnow held the stick, and the man yanked Minnow through the mud another two feet, within his reach. The man dropped the stick and flailed his hand at Minnow, pulling him closer, pulling him down into the mud. He moaned and mumbled and then yelled something, but his mouth was full of mud and the words slurred together into nonsense. Minnow lost the stick and the man had him by the shoulder, pulling him closer, head rolling, gaping scabby hole tilting toward him.

"Stop!"

The man pulled him closer, curling a muscled bicep, squeezing to maintain a grip despite the mud. He was trying to say something, to do something. Minnow's chest sank into the mud, and his stomach was almost buried deep enough to trap him for good. He strained his neck to keep his head up. He beat against the man's shoulder and then tried to turn from his lying position.

Down he went, deeper. He threw his arms out and slapped the muddy flesh. Minnow's face pressed down into the mud. He tasted the salt and it oozed into one nostril. The next lurch would probably put him under. He balled his fist and landed a blow against the man's mud-caked ear, right under the gaping wound. The grip released, and Minnow exploded backwards. He scrambled onto his back, kicking away from the man, splashing back through the trough he'd made. The man gurgled something through his mud-filled mouth, and Minnow kept moving toward the causeway until he felt the first of the tumbledown bricks.

Minnow slathered a hand across his forehead but only spread the mud more. The dog came to him, licking the mud off the side of his face. Minnow eased up to his feet and climbed the ruined slope, up to the highest remaining part of the causeway. He looked back at the man, still waving the one arm, still stuck in the mud. He bent over and put his muddy hands against the sides of his head. He took a deep breath and kept walking down the causeway. He heard more moans, more screams. The screams of a hundred people. But he did not stop.

Gray clouds swept over the bowl of the sky as he walked the last stretch of the ruined causeway. He entered the shredded woods on the other side and the clouds left, swept away by a swift, chilling wind. The road he'd come in on was muddy, narrowed, clogged with flotsam from the flood. He walked with the dog at his side through the sparse forest, looking for the main road.

Broken trees lined the path. The once-thick woods were now empty and hollowed out. The earth was churned into mud, and trees lay scattered like toothpicks. He passed a great live oak uprooted and toppled across the road. Its crown blocked the way, and the hole where its massive root ball had been was big enough to hide a house.

Bodies were strewn along the road, broken and bent and split open. He passed one corpse impaled on a snapped tree trunk, its insides red and shiny. Crows sat in the bare branches overhead and took turns swooping down to pick at the stringy mess.

Standing water slowed their pace. The road was flooded in one place, and Minnow waded through carefully, looking for hazards. He passed several bloated bodies. He saw the first white body in the pool, face down, skin milky and blotched purple. His movement in the water caused it to float away, and when it brushed a stump it made a deep popping noise and released a stench. Minnow held back his vomit and made it out of the water with only muddy ankles.

The road stayed dry for a while, but then it wound into a low hollow that had filled with flood water. The dog sniffed its edges, and Minnow considered the way around. It was bigger than the haunted swamp, even, like a lake right in their path.

"Road's out there somewhere."

Something splashed into the water in front of them, not fifty feet away. A tiny black head emerged on the surface, and the snake swam along with ripples fanning out behind. Minnow heard another splash, and another, and then saw one of them falling: a twisting black rope dropping from the canopy. He turned to the canopy and saw more coiled there, clinging to branches, clustered in the forks of high trunks.

"Look out."

A snake came out of the water next to them and slithered under a fallen log. He watched another snake drop, as big around as his arm. It splashed hard, and he didn't see it surface.

"We're not swimming this."

They walked right, away from the muddy rut of road, careful to avoid the murky edge of the brown flood. They saw more bodies floating in the water, and the bow of a big boat, maybe one of the steamers that ran from Newfort to Savannah. They went far around the flood and found no shallow place to ford, then doubled back and tried the other way. Snakes slithered out of the water, wet and shiny, some whipping injured tails.

The dog nipped at a slow snake, then retreated when it struck back. The dog was skinny, ribs showing, but not much worse than when Minnow had first met him in Port Royal. He thought of the plate of shrimp and wished for breakfast, or lunch, or anything to eat while they walked the lapping edge of the flood.

Finally they came to a place where a pine had snapped in the storm, all the way down by its stump. The tree lay long across the flood, with the thick bottom end on their side and the broken crown on the other.

"Follow me."

Minnow mounted the stump and walked it with his arms out. The rough bark was wet, but still craggy enough for his sandals to find purchase. The dog followed behind, tail wagging, panting, a bit of drool running from its mouth.

They wove through the tangled branches at the other end, and carefully picked past a naked body slumped in the broken limbs. The skin on the feet was missing, showing pink flesh and bits of bone. Minnow hopped down to solid ground, and looked across the brown water. Maybe that was the worst, behind them. He had to find the road, and Frogmore, and get back to Dr. Crow with the dust.

The land dried up as they walked the island's slight elevation. The woods did not seem as ravaged, and for a while he thought that maybe the storm had spared the interior of the islands. Maybe just the outer edges were pounded by the rain, the flood, the terrible wind.

They walked on, leaving Coffin's Point behind. Minnow's legs hurt. Not from injury, but from exhaustion. He'd never walked so many miles in so few days in his life. The next time the gang wanted to take an adventure, he'd probably sit it out. He kept walking, watching his dog. It limped a little, maybe, but it didn't complain.

The woods ended and they found the main road. It was a black-churned highway of mud, trampled by some recent traffic, but empty in every direction. In some places it was washed out entirely, just bare ground strewn with branches and pine needles. In some places it was still a wide, muddy road, ditches intact.

He couldn't tell which way to go, with the road washed out. He knew they had to go south, but the sun was high and he didn't know which way it was falling. Then he spotted another clue: black tendrils curled up above the blasted tree line. Many lines of gray and black, twisting and curling.

"How did it go?" Minnow asked the dog.

Minnow looked up the road, and down the road.

"Chick willa high. Chick willa low."

He looked down the road, at the black in the sky.

"No man can climb chick willa."

They headed that way, the way that had to be south, toward the black in the sky.

"It's smoke," he reminded the dog.

They walked for Frogmore.

They met the first people a few miles out. First a negro woman and her children, slick with mud, walking with blank stares down the middle of the road. The two children were naked, and the woman was covered only by a strip of muddy linen. Minnow tried to catch their eyes, but they continued without pausing or regarding him. Later down he passed a wagon stuck in the mud, mule braying, a skinny negro whipping it with a switch. The negro glared up at Minnow and didn't say a word. More bodies farther in: a pile of them, a dozen at least, and farther down the road a man carrying one back toward the pile with a piece of gray fabric around his face. He passed a group of people in the shredded woods, standing among the snapped pine trees and twisted oaks. They were in a circle, holding hands. That was it. No one else. A mile from one of the biggest towns on the Island, and only a handful of living people were on the road.

They found Frogmore destroyed. Most of the buildings were gone, leaving only a rubble-strewn field of foundations. A few ragged stumps remained of other structures, some wood left, a well-built chimney, an iron pipe jutting from the ground. Dead bodies were everywhere: out in the open, half-hidden in the rubble, splayed out in the sun.

Another man came while Minnow watched. He examined one of the bodies, walked around it, then bent over and crammed his arms underneath. His cheeks puffed out and he hauled the corpse over his shoulder. He left, passing Minnow on the road, heading out in the same direction as the other corpse-bearer.

Minnow spotted smoke coming from a building, and he could smell charred wood and something like melting pitch. Half a dozen people were gathered around another fire, a campfire, on the edge of the ruins. Across the entire wasted town, where the road went on south, only two buildings were still standing, and a man wept over a dead horse.

Minnow went into the wasted town with the dog behind him, darting left and right to sniff at different things. It went up to a body, broken almost in half, pinned under a fallen balcony.

"Stay close," Minnow hissed.

They passed ruined houses and flat foundations. A family of three—husband, wife, and toddler—were busy rifling through one mound of wreckage, picking things from the disaster. An old man sat against a hitching post, half-asleep, his eyes staring at a distant place. Moans and whines came from all over, from beneath rubble and from inside make-shift tents, from nearby and from far away.

The storm had plucked trees from the surrounding forest, and the leftovers were stripped of leaf and limb. Roads went off in all directions, but they were no longer quiet pathways or tidy routes through the trees. Now they were washed-out gutters of mud passing through a desolate thicket of sharp trunks and splintered limbs.

The storm had not spared the interior islands. It had washed out the far islands and covered them with the sea. Then it had brought its winds down through the heart, tearing everything away. The rains had flooded the roads and the world had turned black and wet, even in Frogmore. The town was gone, and—for the first time—Minnow wondered what Bay Street would look like. It was farther in, protected by all the barrier islands, but it still had the river right out front. All the miles of marsh and all those high mud flats might have held back something. But the rain. The wind.

A woman shrieked, and he turned and saw a skinny old lady, white, limping up the road, staggering naked through the mud. Her legs were painted with filth up to her hips, and the rest of her skin was wrinkled and covered in spots. She held out a hand and collapsed forward into the mud. Men ran to help her, but when they turned her over they shrank away. They waited a few moments, and then carried her off.

This had been no summer thunderstorm. It had been something else. He stared up at the sky: blue streaked with gray clouds, still flying fast.

"You sorry bastard," he whispered, and kept on through town.

They passed through the southern part of Frogmore, around where he'd met the woman and the boy and had gotten his first help on the way out. No boy, no woman, no house. No blue bottles humming in the wind. No sweet-grass ladies weaving baskets on the side of the road. No hot shrimp plates. They passed a dead dog, which his dog sniffed, and then they left what remained of Frogmore behind.

The southern road was wide, and it had once been bricked in places with ditches on each side. Now it was a flat muddy waste, a strip of dark brown mess snaking through a torn forest, leading somewhere down the line to Newfort. It looked nothing like it ever had before. Bodies were slumped over in the washed-out ditches. Parts of buildings blocked entire stretches, and they had to walk in the woods to get around. A tug boat lay shattered across another stretch, with flies buzzing around its hatches.

And the smell. Everywhere they went they breathed the smell of rotting meat. The smell of the dump in summer. The smell of maggots, and the sound of flies. Animals and people alike bloated all around them, and the air went noxious with their greasy fumes.

They followed the muddy way south, back toward town, back toward the world. Pillars of smoke rose up before them on the horizon over the weakened tree line. Maybe from downtown. Maybe from Bay Street, or Port Royal. It was hard to tell. Minnow's steps fell a little faster, and his dog kept pace. The smoke made him nervous. He wanted to go.

The road seemed to be leading them up, higher. The forest fell away, and they came to another causeway that broke free from the land to lead across a vast marsh field. This cause-way was intact, higher than the other, and farther inland, stretching like a mud finger across the marsh flat.

His dog smelled it first, while they were still standing before the causeway. It wasn't the sweet sulfur odor of pluff mud. It was the stench of the dead. Minnow caught the breeze and doubled over with his hands on his knees. He retched, but nothing came from his empty stomach. He straightened up and held a hand to his face, as if that would do anything to stop the foul corpse wind.

They moved out onto the causeway under the bright sun, with a blue bowl of sky above. The marsh was summer green but muted by a film of churned-up mud. The bodies were everywhere. He'd seen them on the road, in the woods, and out on the mud flat where they'd still been alive. But here were scores. Hundreds, at second look. They dotted the muddy marsh field like so many dark shells on a beach: men, women, children, animals. Bodies lean and narrow and old, bodies swollen and bloated in the sun. Skin white, black, gray, green. All colors strewn across the churned mud basin. The marsh grass was thick with corpses, and no place in the mud was free of some death, animal or human. Buzzards wheeled overhead, turning in overlapping paths. Now and then one would drop from its gyre and roost in a patch of grass, eyeing some new morsel.

His dog dropped its tail between its legs and froze in place. Minnow took his hand from his mouth and retched again, this time leaving ropes of yellow bile in the mud. He wiped his mouth and squeezed the tears out of his eye and kept walking. His dog followed.

None of the bodies moaned or made noises. They were long gone, their spirits already far away. No shaking or screaming, no calling out for help. Everyone was dead. And too many for any one place. These were dead from every-where, dead from the islands and from Frogmore. From Port Royal and Bay Street. From his street.

They reached the midpoint of the causeway. He quickened his pace and the dog kept up, tail still tucked, a whimper coming with every few strides. It was midday when they reached the far end and walked back onto the muddy road. Minnow did not stop to look back over the marsh.

The road narrowed and wound through another devastated mile of forest. The trees were broken and bent to the ground as if gravity had become too much for them to resist. The road snaked and turned, but the way was always south, south toward town, south toward the river.

The people he passed on the way seemed dazed. Some of them were all right, in dry clothes, rested, moving fast to help someone or escape something, maybe. Many were like faded souls, limping in the ditches, sitting on the side of the muddy path, wandering the forest with grievous injuries that took away their minds. If any of them had come from across the river, from town, he could not know and did not ask.

Minnow had hoped to reach the river quickly. The straight path should have been fast, and they walked and even jogged when the mud was not too thick. Still, the sun had begun to drop toward the tree line and he saw no sign of the river, or even of traffic that might be coming from the ferries. His stomach cramped, and he thought about the last time he'd eaten. On the road, maybe. No, back at the village? They kept on and did not stop.

Night was not far off when they found a boat cast into the woods. The trees had grown a little thicker along that part of the road, and looked even thicker still where the boat had brought down branches, limbs, and trunks. It was short and squat, like a tug or a shrimp boat, but it was neither. Its hull had ruptured, and somehow it had come to rest in the middle of the woods. Minnow looked down the road and then at the boat. His stomach growled, and the dog cocked its head at him.

"What do you think?"

The boat was more likely than anything else, even than back in Frogmore, to have some sort of food on board. Minnow licked his chapped lips and nodded.

"Let's go look."

They left the road and approached the side of the boat. It leaned on one side, away from them, and seemed mostly intact on that side except for a deep crack in the hull. Around the other side the trees grew thicker, and the boat had brought down a tangle of vines and a good-sized pine tree—limbs and needles and all—on top of the whole mess. He saw the hidden spot already, a dark place where the boat blocked sight of the road and the trees and vines covered the view from all else. The only way in was through a shadowy space in the thickets. He led the dog through.

Minnow stood in the shade of the boat and heard something from the road, something creaking. He went around aft and watched a man go by on the road, trying to push an empty wheelbarrow through the muck. If he noticed Minnow or his dog, he didn't make a sign.

Minnow waited for the man to go and then walked along the hull to where it had split. Normally the only way in would be a hatch or two up top, but now there was a fissure in the wood that showed the boat's insides. He peeked his head in and looked both ways, motioning his hand softly to keep the dog at bay while he had the first look. It smelled salty, muddy, and moldy. He would have left the shady cove right then had he seen seen a body, but no remains were inside.

He checked once more for bodies and then slipped into the fissure, walking up the inside of the leaning hull. A bunk was at the bow, and something had been stored on shelves on one side, but that was long gone. A small sack of rice was torn open, crawling with mealworms, perfumed with rot, and useless to eat. He saw one last trunk, a travelling trunk, made of wood with metal bands and a big lock on front. The lock was busted, and the trunk was cracked open. His fingers trembled, and he looked at the dog outside, then back up at the trunk. He could see fabric poking out, showing through the open gap.

"Probably just clothes," he whispered out to the dog. He crossed the unsteady floor and put his hand on top of the chest. It was soaked through. The fabric bulging from inside was soaked and drooping, like guts from a body. He lifted the lid and it fell back and boomed and shook the whole boat. His dog ducked out but then came right back. They both stood very still.

Minnow pulled the fabric out, maybe just an uncut bolt, maybe a curtain or rug. It slithered out on its own once he got it started. He moved another layer of clothes: something with lace, a pair of pants, a belt, suspenders. A wooden box was under that. He sucked in a breath and opened it with shaking fingers, but inside was only ruined, waterlogged cigars. He cast the box aside and peered in further, pulling out a soaking felt coat with shiny brass buttons. Under that he found a sodden book, a smaller wooden box, a bottle of wine, a smaller glass bottle, and two cans. A little silver opener lay across the can lids.

He wanted to shove his hands in and take it all, but he froze. He glanced over his shoulder at the dog, who stood sniffing the moldy air. He watched the crack in the hull for any sign of intruders. Minnow took two slow breaths and turned to the trunk. The wine bottle looked old, and the wine appeared brown through the foggy green glass. The other jar was filled with something clear, maybe water, maybe packed for a long journey. He put the opener in his pocket and took the two cans: smoked sardines. He took the wooden box out. Probably ruined inside, but when he undid the clasp and opened it the insides were dry, sealed with a rubber lining. Flint. A block of flint, and a striker, too. He glanced at the dog and smiled.

He built a fire in the shelter between the boat and the trees. Dark was approaching when he first left the shady cove to get kindling. He brought back two armloads and checked to be sure his hiding place was invisible from the outside. The fire and the smoke would show, but nothing could help that.

"We have to have a fire," he said to the dog.

This was the first night after the storm. He thought about all those bodies. All the bodies on the marsh, and the death wind, and the men and women flailing in the mud. He thought about the long road he'd walked, and about how many spirits and souls would be out wandering that night.

"We have to have a fire."

He built it and fanned it and sat against the hull with the dog right next to him. He took off his sandals and crossed his legs and laid his possessions out before the fire: his billfold, his dime, and the goofer dust most important of all. Dr. Crow had better have flown high over the storm to still be there. If Dr. Crow was not there, maybe at least his shack would be, and Minnow would find what he needed and leave the dust as payment.

"He'll be there. Newfort is inland. It's not Frogmore."

He stroked the dog. They watched the fire, both warm and dry by the time the sun set and the night fell over them like a black, muggy blanket. Frogs called out to each other from a hundred hiding places, and the woods were alive with the buzzing and chirping of every bug on the Island. Minnow uncorked the wine with the can opener and opened the first can of sardines. He ate them quickly, with his fingers, gobbling them up and drinking the juice after. He wiped his chin and took a sip of the wine. Thick, red, bitter, and sour in his throat. He took three full gulps and winced against the flavor, but it warmed him better than the sardines. He wiped his hands on his shirt and opened the other can. He ate this one slowly, savoring each slender salty fish, licking his fingers after each one, letting the smoky flavor melt into his tongue. He gave the last two to his dog, and drank the juice himself. He offered the dog some wine, but it turned its nose.

"We may need the water for later."

The dog didn't seem to mind, but Minnow found a bent copper kettle in the boat and filled it halfway with the water. The dog stood and approached quickly, tail wagging, but then turned away at the sight of it, whimpering once and then circling down to bed. Minnow nudged the water toward the dog, but he did not respond.

"Suit yourself."

Minnow poured the water back in the jar, and rubbed his fingers in the sardine can for any last taste of juice.

He cleared a spot just inside the crack in the hull where he could sleep with the boat over his head. The moldy stench was not so bad just inside, where fresh air and a taste of the fire could still reach. He found a thin scrap of fabric that had already dried, and rolled it into a pillow. He stretched out with his arms behind his head, the dog snoring at his side, his mind heavy from the meal and the wine. The orchestra of the woods played on for him, and he tried to see stars through the tattered canopy. A soft wind blew outside, rocking the limbs over his head.

He dreamed of the storm, terrible and angry and beating against him in the tree. He saw the boy's face, and the boy's mother. He heard the house explode and mix with the thunder and the roar of the sea beneath them. He imagined falling from the limb, the rope giving, and hitting that cold ocean water. It would carry him away in a second, washed out with all the debris, all the bodies. He would be stuck in the mud like those people. Naked, mud-covered, helpless.

He dreamed about his dog. He dreamed that his father really liked the dirty mutt.

Minnow opened his eye to a pink dawn splashed with red. He'd slept through the night, harder than he had slept since being in his own bed. The world was quiet, except for a rooster crowing far away. The dog cocked his head at that. Minnow yawned and sat up on his elbows.

"We better go."

He searched for anything useful in the boat, but he didn't want to dig too deeply. He took the jar of water, and they were on the road quickly, leaving a smoldering pile of coals. They would walk fast, not stopping, not eating, not doing anything until they got to the river and could cross home to his family. They set a good pace, but the dog lagged behind.

More traffic was on the road, now, but still no wagons, no carts. Just people walking, most of them with loads on their backs or injured people in their arms. He wanted to ask if anyone had come from town, but their heads were down, their eyes steely. The road widened, and the woods were gone again, with only torn stumps and fallen trunks left behind. They'd reached the exposed edge of the Island, the river, the ferries, and the coast that looked out to Bay Street.

Black smoke billowed in the distance, across the river. Five columns rose from different places: three from Bay Street, one from farther back, and another from around the curve of the land at Port Royal. He breathed out a soft breath when he saw buildings still standing on Bay Street, still lining the water. All of them had seen the storm: roofs were missing, frames were leaning. One building was gone altogether, but he could not tell which. It left a tooth-gap in the line of buildings on the water. People swarmed around, only black ants to him from across the marsh and the broad river. He moved his gaze to Port Royal, which showed only as a white sandy line from his vantage point.

"Dr. Crow," he said.

He saw no boats. The river would normally be filled with shrimp boats returning to Port Royal, with dinghies ferrying people back and forth to anchored sailboats. The river would be crossed by the paths of a half-dozen ferries, including the one that had brought him from Port Royal. Including Calico Jack's. But no pleasure crafts were there, no rowboats on the mudflats. No one casting nets or fishing on the marsh's edge. Just bodies floating amid debris. Pieces of buildings, roofs, boats, shingles, and pilings. Entire boats upside down. Barges cast adrift, spinning across the river on the incoming current. But no boats in action. No one on the water, alive.

The coast right in front of him, the southern end of the Island, was stripped bare. Wind or waves had carved away a large portion of the bluff, and the land between the water's edge and where he stood was a washed-out swath of sand and tree stumps, with nothing but a few brick foundations to mark any sign of former civilization. Dozens of docks might have once lined the shore there, and twice as many boat landings. Boats would be coming and going from that shore all day long. Now it was a raw, blasted coastline, dotted with bodies blackened in the sun, buzzing with flies.

Minnow ran to the bluff's broken edge, kneeling down in the mud to look out at the river beyond. He wanted to call out to Bay Street, to scream and see if any of his friends could hear him, or if his mother or father would know his voice. Instead he just looked out over the slate gray river, with his dog at his side. A stiff breeze came blowing across, somehow cold despite the summer sun, somehow raw after the storm.

"We have to cross it."

He'd crossed so many streams and creeks and rivers on his journey. He'd seen many spans of water and mud and found ways each time. But this was a big river, the Newfort River, and it swirled deep and wide with wreckage from the storm. The tide drew inward, with water flowing in from his right. If he crossed right there, in front of Bay Street, he would be sucked farther down toward Port Royal. And maybe that's what he needed. The goofer dust would do him no good on Bay Street. He needed the medicine.

A loud noise came across river, shaking him even so far away. He heard faint yelling from across the water, then saw part of a building fall. Dust billowed up, and then a new chimney of smoke rose like a finger. He thought of his little house, a few blocks away from whatever had happened. He wondered if their roof had stayed on, if his father was dry, if his mother needed help, now, too.

"We have to be quick."

He moved down to a stretch of sand scattered with debris, including a wagon and a bloating body. He shook his head to clear the image and tried to think of the place as it would have been just a few days ago: busy, bright, people everywhere, pack animals pulling wagons and hauling loads, ferries coming and going.

"Come on."

He led his dog up to the wagon, but the dog hesitated and moved slowly. Minnow did not wait for it to keep up. No time for that.

The wagon was empty. Some of the contents had spilled out of the broken hatch on top. The inside had been picked bare, though, by something or someone. The hatch that had covered the top entry to the wagon lay upside down next to one of the cracked wheels. The hatch was the size of a small table, and its inside edges had been padded with soft fabric bumpers.

"Might float all right," Minnow said. Most of all, it was big enough for both of them.

He gazed out over the river. It was dark, and coming in fast, swirling with wreckage. He knew he could make it. He could set off right from where they were and just paddle straight ahead, letting the current land them farther down the bank on the other side, closer to Port Royal.

He dragged the hatch to the bluff, checked its physical soundness, and then let it tumble down the bluff end-over-end. If it broke on the way down, it wasn't meant for a raft anyway. The crosshatch of boards and bumpers held together, and all he needed was a paddle to guide them. He returned to the wagon and found nothing, then investigated closer around the dead driver and came up empty. They went down the bluff and searched the muddy edge next to the water. Some driftwood. Planks, rough and useless. Then he found a piece of an oar, just a foot of splintered handle and a half-broken paddle. A heavy bolt stuck out of the handle, almost at the end, where it might have once held the oar in a lock.

They didn't even go back up. Minnow could hardly keep his eye off the river, off the coast on the other side, off the tiny black shapes of people moving, searching, working on the shore beyond. He stepped carefully along the slimy edge of mud, his dog behind him, to where their raft sat on its edge by the water.

He flipped it over into the mud and pushed it out into the water a bit with his foot. The near edge stayed stuck.

"Come on," he said to the dog.

The dog cocked its head, used its paw to knock a bit of drool off its upper lip, then hopped on to the raft. It cowered at the sight of the water, tail between its legs, ears pinned back. It had swum enough on the trip, escaping currents and tides and storms and even a plateye. Maybe it had finally had enough.

Minnow looked up at the bluff, then down the length of the muddy shore. He'd been long on the Island, and the islands beyond, but now was the time to cast off. Time to head home. The dog hunkered down low on the hatch, and Minnow knelt and pushed off with one leg. The raft broke free of the mud and drifted into an open shallow flanked by tall marsh grass. He lay down on his stomach and scooted forward so that his face was flush with the front and his toes just hung off the back edge. He paddled from there.

His short paddle reached the bottom, at first, pressing into the soft pluff mud that was just visible through the tea-colored water. He pushed along through the shallows, past the ruined timbers of a dock, past pieces of what might have been a flat-bottomed ferry. The marsh dwindled on either side, but still he pushed through the shallows.

Then the mud dropped beneath them. The world fell away and the water turned black under the little raft. The current caught them, pushing just slightly against their starboard side. The dog scooted to that side and growled at the water. Minnow paddled on the left and kept them carefully on course. He checked their bearing and then stared down at the inky depths below. The mast of a sailboat passed just under their raft, a gray shadow in the dark water. He thought of the bodies and skeletons down there, the jagged shipwrecks and pieces of houses flung into the deep by the storm. He checked to make sure his feet weren't dangling over the edge and paddled on.

They were a quarter of the way across, with the marsh well behind, when the dog jumped. A wheel and axle from a wagon went spinning by in the water, twirling in an eddy. The wheel missed them, but it spooked the dog and he jumped from the raft into the river. Minnow hardly looked. He just kept rowing at the water with his paddle. The dog had swum well enough before, and it had the raft to return to if it tired.

The current drifted them left, the raft eased down the river, with the dog paddling after. He could hear it, but he did not look back. That dog had survived the storm, the plateye, the marshes, and the rivers. By rights it should already have been dead. It could do one more swim, surely.

They weren't halfway across yet, but Bay Street had grown much clearer. He could see rents in the buildings where walls had given in to wind, and tumbledown places where roofs had caved under the weight of the downpour. People moved around, some running, some gathering in groups, some wandering slowly behind the buildings where the water met the land.

The current took them left, still facing Bay Street right on, but drifting steadily to port. Port Royal was way down the river that way, a ruined white mess. The dog was behind him, starboard, he could hear, and Bay Street was still straight ahead.

He pulled at the water with his paddle, then brought it up and stroked again. He struggled through a raft of dried spartina, set free on the river by the high tide and the night wind, and beyond the spartina through a line of three bodies. He couldn't tell if they were colored or white, men or women. The skin was gray and puffy and wrinkled, and in some places it had gone soft, and bone showing beneath the rotting flesh. Minnow looked up and scanned the river.

Halfway across, and they were the only ones on the water. Not another raft, not another dinghy, not another boat. It looked like some crafts were up on the bluff, at some places, but they were all crowded by people, under repair, grounded by the storm. No one out there noticed him. No one on land could even see them among the flotsam. He thought of calling out, but instead he just rowed the raft ever closer to shore.

He did not hear the dog now. Maybe it had been caught up in the dried spartina, or the float of bodies. A cold spot burned in his heart when he thought that maybe it had gotten tired. Maybe it had drowned. Minnow was tired himself. He'd crossed a lot of water, and yet this last stretch seemed to exhaust him more than any. The dog was probably hungry, hurt, weak. Minnow could not hear its ragged panting, or its rough paddling, or any signal that it was still alive.

He pulled in his makeshift oar and put it on the raft, careful not to let it roll off. He looked at Bay Street one more time, then turned on his side to look back. His dog was there. It had fallen a few feet behind but was still paddling strong.

"Come on. We're so close." Minnow threw a hand up at Bay Street, trying to show the dog how near they were.

The dog paddled normally for another moment, then sank lower in the water. Minnow rose to his knees, wondering how he might help the animal get on board. Then the dog moved faster, gliding along the surface, somehow barely paddling while still making up the distance with new speed. It strained its neck to keep its head clear of the water and bared its teeth to show more drool.

"Come on!" Minnow called.

At first he thought the drool was from exhaustion. Then he saw the curdled foam clinging to the dog's black lips. The foam webbed when it chomped its jaws, and from that white mess came the strings of slobber. The dog was sick. Minnow didn't understand, at first. He rolled on his back and instinctively drew his legs away from the approaching animal. Then he remembered, and knew. Rabies.

The dog was ten feet off now and coming fast. Minnow moved onto his haunches, balanced out like a perfect scale, raft rocking beneath him.

"Get!"

The dog kept coming, neck strained forward, eyes rolling back and forth in its head as its tongue lolled through the white foam.

"Get!"

It paddled faster now, approaching the raft, pawing and splashing at the water as it drew closer. Minnow took up the oar and moved to row for Bay Street, but it was too late. The dog was almost on him. He brandished the oar like a baseball bat instead.

He hefted his weapon and felt its weight, then the dog howled and launched itself onto the raft. For a second its eyes locked on Minnow, and they looked brown and human and angry. Minnow swung the oar and pushed out with his feet at the same time. The dog was right on him, but his blow connected. He lunged backward at the same time, sending the raft away with his feet. He splashed in and lost the oar. The cold, salty water took him and he squeezed his eye shut and blew bubbles from his nostrils to stop the water from coming in. He thought he might gasp in fear and drown himself, and then he thought the dog was on him again and would bite him in the river.

He tore his way to the surface and slathered the water off of his good eye. He blinked and saw the raft rocking in his wake. The dog lay on it, convulsing and whimpering in seizure. Drool pooled at its open mouth, and then dark red blood. It snapped at the air and howled. Then it lay still.

Minnow swam in place, watching the raft to be sure. Rabies took a long time to show. Dogs that might have it had to be killed right away, else risk spreading it to another creature or human. How long had his dog festered?

The dog was not dead yet. It lifted its head and howled one more time: a human scream that was high pitched, like a last breath escaping through a reed-tight airway. It convulsed again, rolled, and splashed into the water. The body floated for a moment, then sank into the depths.

For a moment Minnow did not move. He floated motionless in the water, arms stiff, mouth agape, eye frozen on the dark place where the dog had gone under. Then he sank, and the air in his lungs was not enough to keep him up. He went under for just a second and then sprang to life, paddling himself up to the surface. He spun in the river to get his bearings, and saw Bay Street ahead, the place where the steep bluff led up to the big mansions that overlooked the bend in the river. He swam, not looking back at the raft.

The path through the water in front of him seemed clear. No debris, no wreckage except maybe straight ahead where the water met the bluff. He swam closer now, making long strokes, sandals still on, giving him an extra strength against the water. He licked his salty lips, kept his head up, and paddled for the bluff, alone.

He passed a half-sunken sailboat moored out in front of the bluff, and then he hit the outer edges of a thin bank of marsh grass that spread out from the land. The water got warmer at the edge, and he could see islands of grass as he swam. Soon the bottom came up beneath him and he grazed it with his sandals. He'd come up centered on the steep grassy bluff that he'd passed along so many days ago.

The mansions were still there, columns still standing, but their roofs torn away. Chimneys were tumbled, and outbuildings and sheds were gone. Fences were scattered like toothpicks, and debris and wreckage lay everywhere, blown by the wind. A few people moved up along the road at the top of the bluff, a few people milled around near the mansions. Most of the traffic and chaos was down on his right, toward Bay Street's cobblestones.

He put his legs down, his sandals pressed into the sandy mud bottom, and he was back. He swam with his hands and kicked off the bottom until the water was only up to his bellybutton. He passed a dead body, gray and bloated, face up, mouth hanging open. Then another. Then he pressed through a line of corpses, floating together, wrinkled and faceless, some with the bones of their skulls showing. He had to push one out of the way to get by.

The water warmed, now at his knees, then down to his ankles. He collapsed forward onto the muddy base of the bluff. He crawled up a few feet and bowed down as if in prayer, clutching the tendrils of centipede grass in his tired hands. He dragged himself up and then crawled to where it was dry.

A voice called down from the top of the incline, from the road.

"Hey!"

Minnow looked up but did not see anyone. He heaved in a breath and looked over his shoulder, back at the river, to the Island beyond, now only a green line of trees.

"Hey, kid!"

A skinny man with a patchy beard appeared at the top of the bluff. He cocked his head, watched Minnow for a moment, and then came scrambling down the grassy hill.

"You all right? You come out the river?"

Minnow nodded, and the man was on him, hands on his shoulders, standing him up. Minnow could barely stay on his feet, and the man struggled to drag him up the bluff.

"Were you out there in the storm?"

The man took him up to the washed-out road. He appraised Minnow, considering his odd sweet grass sandals, his tattered pants, and his threadbare shirt. He looked at Minnow's one eye, and the patch, and winced.

"Did you hear me? Were you out in the storm? How long you been out there?"

Minnow leaned down on his knees and looked at the solid ground under his feet. He straightened and gazed out over the river from the vantage of the bluff. When he squinted, he felt his skin cracked and burned from long days under the sun.

"Are you all right, boy?" The man's eyes were wide, his mouth ajar like he was studying some strange specimen.

Minnow nodded, and the man stood there watching him. A crash came from the direction of Bay Street. The man shook his head, muttered something under his breath, and ran off toward the calamity. Minnow's path was the other way. Home was Bay Street, back to the road that would take him to his father, his mother. Still there. He was sure. The house would be there. Newfort had been spared the worst. Everything in him pulled his body toward Bay Street, but he could not go. He looked back at the Island and then broke into a run, away from town, running for Port Royal.

He did not want to go there. Not after crossing the river and killing his dog. Not after the Island and all those tiny islands out there on the verge of the ocean. He wanted to go back down Bay, past the places he knew and the shops he'd recognize, even if they were falling down—even though they were broken and cracked and changed. But he couldn't.

He ran, now, past the tall white roofless mansions. One of them had burned to the ground, and another was half-burned. He wanted to stop and see, to see the rich mansions he knew so well now made into hovels. But he couldn't. He didn't have time. He had to find Crow.

He left the bluff and tore down the muddy forest road. It was not much different than out on the Island: forest shredded, thinned, wasted since he'd walked through it days ago. No bodies. Plenty of dead animals: a field of dead cows, a dog in a tree, but no dead people. His feet pained him as he ran. While his legs had ached from exhaustion, his feet hurt more acutely. The sandals had taken him well, but each foot had a bruised place where bone had met hard ground far too many times. Each step was a burst of pain, but still he ran.

Sparse living traffic made way as he pushed through: a crowd of children led by a woman in a white dress, two men stumbling arm-in-arm, a bare-chested negro carrying a corpse on his shoulder. The world had been torn by the storm, and people were only just starting to emerge from the cracks and breaks to see what had gone wrong.

He passed a few intersections in the road, a few forks, and then no people at all. He knew he was on the right path, but no one was going his way. No one was going to or coming from the busiest port for miles. He emerged from the trees and saw why. Port Royal was a wasted hell.

The buildings were gone. Even more than in Frogmore, everything was gone. The town of whitewashed planks and unsanded timbers had been wiped out, as if by a tidal wave. The boards coated the ground like a carpet of bleached wood, even and flat all the way to the river except where it lumped over the remains of larger structures or other debris. The docks were gone, the buildings were gone. What remained was only a treeless, planked cove on the desolate river, with a winding mud road going back to town. The planks baked under the high sun, and the place reeked like rotting meat. Dogs chased each other from place to place, and people were everywhere.

Some were trapped, calling out. Screams came from mounds of debris and planks. A big muscled white man had a colored man by both hands, trying to pull him out from under the wreckage. The negro screamed and screamed. Minnow began walking through the wreckage, craning his neck to look for Crow's shack on the far beach.

Two men on the eastern edge of the clearing had a woman pinned down, wrestling with her. Another woman wept over a dead goat. The goat stank, Minnow could smell, even as he passed them by in the road. Everything was strange, different, flattened. No shrimp, no singing, no dancing in halls behind closed doors. The woman wailed over her animal, and a man called out in the distance. Reports rocked the air, one after the other, a half-dozen gunshots. He went on, passing over a dozen different dead men and one dead woman. They stank, and they were bloated, and their eyes were gray or just empty sockets where fiddler crabs had eaten the soft parts.

He knew the shack was gone before he got to the beach. The whole town was gone, but he had held hope until he was really there, standing on the oyster beach where the shack had been. Maybe not right there, but somewhere close. He'd hoped for a pile of rubble to search. Maybe the chest was still there, or the shelf with all the medicine. Maybe Crow was still there with his treasures to save his father.

But nothing remained. Only dead people, crying women, and the birds eating the bodies. He would have fallen to his knees to weep, but the oyster shells would have cut him. He bit his lip and squeezed his good eye shut. When he opened it, the shack was still gone. As if it had never been there. He put his hand through his hair, almost dry now, gritty with sand, tangled into locks.

Minnow dug into his pocket and took out the leather pouch. The dirt inside was soaked, packed inside like a clump of beach sand. The grave dust would do him no good, now, without Crow to make the exchange. He loosened the drawstring and dumped the little clump out onto the oyster rake, where it blended in with everything else. He stubbed at it with his foot and heaved in one sobbing breath. He thought about Crow, and about Sorry George. The three things. He thought about his dog.

A sound came from the water then again: the spray from a dolphin's blowhole, blasting out a plume of foam and air. A pod swam the river, still alive, blowing spouts but showing only the slick gray tops of their bodies as they went along under the water. A dozen, two dozen, moving together in rhythm through the river. The debris out there was easy for them to get around, and they glided free in water empty of boats and docks.

He thought of his house, his father, his mother. And he ran. He ran out of the ruined port, he ran back to the bluff, by the houses, to Bay Street.

The street was a mess, strewn with debris and wreckage, clogged with people and animals on the move. The rain—and maybe even the flood, if it had gotten high enough—had washed up cobblestones and left some places only bare mud. The cleanup had begun in many places, and dazed men worked at shop fronts and on the roofs of buildings, making rough emergency repairs. Other buildings were abandoned, dark, gutted by the wind, with no one attending. One building had burned to the ground, leaving an empty gap close to the river. No structure was unharmed. Everything had been touched by the storm. Smoke, rotting meat, sewage. The air reeked. A man lay over a dead horse, crying.

Minnow came to Ander's, where his journey had begun so many days before. The big glass front was shattered, and two giant beams had fallen in from the roof and smashed the interior. The storm had destroyed the store. He turned to leave and saw the pharmacist crouched down at the corner of the building. His back was turned, and his clothes were stained with mud.

Minnow looked up Bay Street, then back down. He adjusted his eye patch and walked up behind the pharmacist. He tapped him on the shoulder, and the man turned and stood up. He looked around, over Minnow's head at first, and then noticed the boy standing in front of him.

"What do you want?" the pharmacist asked. He had one cut across his forehead, but he otherwise looked the same.

"I want my money. Or I want my medicine."

"Money? Medicine? Are you all right, boy?"

The pharmacist leaned in and tried to touch Minnow's patch, but Minnnow put his hand up and grabbed the man's wrist.

"My eye is fine."

Minnow squeezed, and the pharmacist withdrew his hand. Then the man's eyes widened. He opened and closed his mouth without speaking. It was like he'd found a strange specimen in a carnival sideshow.

"You sent me to Crow," Minnow said. "And he sent me out to the islands. I finished my part of the deal."

"Your eye."

"I want medicine for my father."

The pharmacist patted his chest and his pockets with his hands absently, as if half asleep. He looked at Minnow, streaked with mud, hair matted, skin pink, patch across his eye.

"The money is gone," the man finally said, gesturing at his ruined store. The pharmacist took a step back and stumbled over a loose cobblestone.

Minnow clenched his fists.

"You're going to help me."

The man looked at him. He stared into Minnow's eye and then looked up, scanning the busy street. Then he spun around, frantic almost, and gazed into the rubble of the store. He crouched down and entered through the broken front window. Minnow watched him stumble around shattered glass and fallen boards, and then finally stoop at a pile of bottles and vials that had been swept together on the muddy floor.

"What are you doing?" Minnow asked.

The pharmacist picked through the pile, throwing broken shards over his shoulder, tossing shattered bottles aside. Then he picked up a muddy flask. He spit on it, rubbed the mud off the glass, and came back out.

"Here," he said, holding the dirty bottle out to Minnow.

Minnow took the vial and examined it. A picture of an Indian was on the front, and a little cork sealed the top. The liquid inside was thin and brown.

"This isn't it," Minnow said.

"It'll help him. He'll feel better," the pharmacist said. A little grin flashed across his face, and Minnow glared at him. The pharmacist noticed, and let out a soft laugh.

"He'll feel as good as anyone here," he said, laughing again, wiping a hand across his face, smearing mud. The laughter turned to sobbing, and he held his head in his hands and cried.

"Thank you," Minnow said, but the pharmacist didn't look up. "Now I have to go home."

HE RAN, AND NO ONE stopped him. He saw nobody he knew, and he thought only briefly of his gang and where they might be. He kept his head up and kept moving. He kept the medicine safe, clutched in his hand.

He turned north on the road that would take him home. He'd walked that road many days ago, and now he was on it again, in a different world. He turned down his street and saw his house, and it was intact. Some of the shingles on top had peeled away at one corner. Trash and debris had blown all across the yard and across the road. But his house was still standing. He ran across the yard and kicked off his sweetgrass sandals along the way. He went up the stoop and flung the door open without even stopping to listen for his mother, or his father.

"Mama!" His voice cracked at the word.

He plunged down the hallway, dark wood and dim light, and turned the corner into his parents' room. The space was bright compared to the rest of the house, and he saw his mother's shape first: a black silhouette against the yellow light from the window. A hand went to her mouth. His father was there in the bed, with the sheet pulled up to his chest. But something was different.

Minnow stumbled into the room. His mother took a step back, and her face twisted at the sight of him. He fell into her arms and she hugged him, locking her hands at the nape of his neck. His skin, burned pink from the sun, hurt where her hands touched. Then he pushed away to see the bed.

His father's eyes were open, and he had turned his head to see them embrace. His face was gaunt, eyes hollow, but Minnow saw life.

"Daddy," Minnow whispered. His mother released him, and Minnow swayed on his feet. He held out the medicine.

"I brought this. It will help you."

His father smiled. The smile was slow, and weak, and his lips moved to whisper. Minnow approached him softly, carefully.

His father lifted a hand from beneath the sheet and touched Minnow's arm, when he was close enough.

"Thank you," he said.

Tears washed over Minnow's vision, and he nodded.

"I went a long way," Minnow said.

His father closed his eyes, breathed, and then opened them again.

"I dreamed of you," his father said. "There was a dog, too."

Minnow smiled and his mother hugged him. He looked up at her, and she put a hand on his eye patch. Her face broke from relief to dismay.

"Your eye," she whispered.

"It's fine now."

"No," she said, putting her hands on his shoulders.

Minnow imagined what she saw: her son skinnier by pounds, clothed in rags, legs scabbed, hair in damp tangles. He swallowed and his throat hurt.

"The storm," she said. "How are you alive?"

Minnow thought back to the live oak he'd clung to in the rain and the woman who had not lived.

"You made me strong," he said. He had no other answer to give.

"Tell us what happened," she said.

"I will. I'll tell you everything."

Acknowledgments

✹

THANKS TO THE South Carolina Arts Commission and The Humanities Council SC for their support of the South Carolina First Novel Prize, and to Ben Fountain for judging the 2014 competition.

Thanks to C. Michael Curtis for working with me to make *Minnow* a better book, and to all the folks at the Hub City Writers Project—especially Betsy Teter—for guiding me through the publication process.

Thanks to Lucy Davey for creating a beautiful illustration that captures so much of the story in a single work of art. Thanks to Meg Reid for her professional design on the book, website, and more.

Thanks to all of my coworkers at Polo Road Elementary— and all the media specialists in Richland 2—for teaching me that excellence comes from pushing yourself and stretching your limits.

Thanks to my brother and my sisters, who each laid a unique stepping stone in the path that led me to writing. Thanks to my parents for guiding me on that path—especially through the hard parts.

Thanks to my wife, Jess, who will always be my first reader, my best friend, and my true love.